Struggle Between Two Lives

Struggle Between Two Lives

Struggle Between Two Lives

Struggle Between Two Lives

© Copyright 2022 Lena Ma

Cover Design by Cover Couture
www.bookcovercouture.com

Struggle Between Two Lives

Table of Contents

Table of Contents

Chapter One

Redeemer Elementary School was a wide gray brick building, square with a flat roof, like someone had designed a child's plastic block. You could almost imagine the brief: keep it simple, square, don't overwhelm the little kids with unusual shapes and embellishments because they are there to learn. This, coupled with the fact that my father's favorite saying, on the rare occasions that he opened his mouth to offer us his wisdom, was *Rules equal success*, made the butterflies in my stomach swarm like bees around pollen.

I had yet to work out how rules equated to success. I followed all my parents' rules, and yet, they never once congratulated me on my success at being a good daughter.

A rusty metal sign hung above the school's entrance; it read *God First*, and then the school's name. It was a Catholic school, which meant that it was strict, religious, and same-sex, my parent's top choice for an education that would ensure their daughter spent her time studying and not associating with boys.

I tried to be excited; I really did. This was my first step on the path to becoming one of those girls I watched on TV, a girl who went to classes clutching her books to her chest, wore short skirts and long socks, laughed a lot, played basketball, and drank milkshakes at the diner after school.

But the weight of learning to speak English fluently so that I could teach my mother pressed heavily on my shoulders. She hadn't expressed in words that there was a timescale on achieving this fluency, but my seven-year-old brain had attached its own time limit to the task. It was almost, *teach me to speak like a regular American before you reach high school, or I will spontaneously self-combust.* It was a big ask of a little girl.

Of course, my father could never do it himself. He was always working long shifts, barely making any time for any of us. He was an American, fluent in the skill, but there was just always that disconnect that made the rest of us feel detached from him.

The other girls hugged their moms at the school gate, the moms waiting with their hands raised until their daughters were swallowed up by the stark gray building. Some knelt on the floor, kissed their daughters' forehead, and smoothed their bright blonde hair away from their face, before saying, "Have a good day, sweetheart."

My mom waited, without touching me, for the door to open and a teacher to appear, hands by her side, avoiding eye contact with anyone, including her own daughter. When the children started filtering through the gates, turning, and waving goodbye, my mom said, "Be good, Yù." And then she walked away.

I took a deep breath, pushed my tiny, black-rimmed glasses further up my nose, and walked through the door to the main reception. I stood on tiptoes so that I could speak to the woman at the desk, and even then, she still had to lean forward to see me properly. Her strawberry-blonde hair was like a bird's nest. Her glasses were pushed up into her hair, gold chains swinging from both sides of her face.

"Hello, miss," I said. "I'm new here. My name is Jade Xiu."

The lady chewed her gum, her lips twisted to one side, and her tongue smacking against her teeth. My mother would have been horrified. I was fascinated. I watched as she typed a few words on her keyboard and peered at me again over the side of the counter.

"Jade Xiu," she confirmed as if I'd mispronounced my own name. "Now, where are you from, Jade Xiu?"

"Philadelphia, miss," I replied.

"No, where are you *really* from?" She lowered her glasses onto the bobble of her nose and stared at me from behind thick lenses.

"Uh," I was confused by the question. Did she want me to tell her my address? "I was born in Philadelphia," I said.

"Okay." The woman sighed and rolled her eyes as if I were making the conversation awkward for her. "But where are you *really* from?"

I had never been asked that question before. I rarely spoke to anyone apart from my parents, but I had never heard them answer this question before either, even though my mother was *really* from China and not Philadelphia. I felt as if I were under attack. But it was my first day at school, and I didn't want to give the wrong first impression. I knew my parents would be livid if they were told that I had disrespected an elder.

So, I said the only thing I could think of on the spot. "My mom came from China, miss. My dad was born here."

She settled back in her seat, a smile on her face. "I'm Miss Genevieve," she said. "Here is your class schedule."

She handed me a sheet of paper with the days broken into square chunks with class names inserted, and then pointed me in the direction of my first class.

My heart thumped crazily as I walked to the appointed room. I was smart, so I didn't fear the schoolwork. It was the students I was afraid of. I nervously twisted the brass doorknob when I reached Mr. Matthews' math class, took a deep breath, and waited for my heartbeat to stop telling me to turn around and run away. If the children behind the door were being noisy, I would not have heard them over the sound of my own blood rushing through my veins.

I opened the door. To my surprise, there were only a few children in the class, and even the teacher had yet to show up. Relieved, my body sagged visibly, my shoulders drooped, and I stepped quietly inside and made my way to the back of the room where I found an empty desk by the window. I made myself comfortable, setting my pencil, ruler, and eraser in the center of the desk, and waited patiently for class to start.

I sensed eyes on me, but I focused on the board fixed to the wall at the front of the class, too afraid to make a sudden movement in case someone pounced on me. Some girls whispered behind my back, their fingers pointed in my direction. I tried to ignore the sound of hissing snakes, but it was difficult when the hissing was crawling all over my skin like a rash. I thought that these girls did not grow up with manners like Joseph and me. My mother would have punished me for being so rude.

I was grateful when I heard the bell ringing in the distance, and Mr. Matthews walked through the door. My cheeks were hot and pink, and I felt as though I needed a drink of water. Everyone turned to face the front of the class, and the whispering snakes vanished as though I had imagined them.

While I was happy that the teacher did not make me stand in front of the whole class and introduce myself, part of me was disappointed that he didn't suggest another girl for me to work with on my first day. So, I kept my head down and concentrated on Mr. Matthews' every word.

When he suggested that we spend the last fifteen minutes of the class working on the three questions he had written on the board, everyone gathered in pairs, their wavy blonde heads nudged together. My brown locks stood out like a sore thumb.

I tried to block out the sounds of their conversations and chewed the end of my pencil while I worked out the questions that had been set. I heard footsteps approaching and glanced up to find Mr. Matthews sliding into the empty desk beside me.

He smiled, said, "Hi, Jade," and offered me his hand to shake.

"Hello," I said back.

"I'm Mr. Matthews. I know how difficult it can be starting a new school when you don't know anyone. If you need help with anything, please don't be afraid to come and speak to me."

Mr. Matthews had kind blue eyes, brown wavy hair that framed his face, and a warm energy about him that instantly made me feel comfortable. I wished, right then and there, that he would be my teacher from now until I started college.

He walked back to the front of the class, and everyone's head turned in my direction. A few of the girls snickered. It wasn't until the bell rang announcing second period, that I finally understood the meaning of *Saved by the Bell*.

By lunchtime, I felt like a fish who had leapt out of a pond and onto Main Street, flapping about and with no clue where I should go to eat, so I followed the other girls, pretending that I knew exactly where I was going. The cafeteria was small with connecting rooms for the students to mingle. It smelled of cleaning products and ketchup, and I almost slipped on the shiny tiled floor.

When my mother set out my clothes for school that morning, she told me to focus on my studies and avoid making friends.

"Friends only slow you down, so don't bother with them."

I didn't know how to tell her that I was desperate to make friends, to have someone to share secrets and laughter with, so I simply nodded.

Remembering her words now, I did not attempt to sit next to anyone. I sat at an empty table and opened my lunchbox.

This was the moment when I realized that I was unlike any of these other girls. I opened my lunchbox to reveal steamed noodles and dumplings, a bean pancake, and chopsticks. Without moving my head, I glanced sideways at the table closest to me and saw that the children had sandwiches made with thin white bread and cut into trim triangular quarters. They had apples and bananas. Some had sticks of carrot. Whatever foods the other girls had did not smell of soy sauce, green onions, and chili.

Everyone watched me as I picked up the noodles with my chopsticks and raised them to my mouth as though I was an alien from a different universe. I could have packed up my lunchbox and moved to a connecting room, but then everyone would have known how much their stares and pointing fingers bothered me, so I stayed at that table and ate my noodles until they made me feel sick.

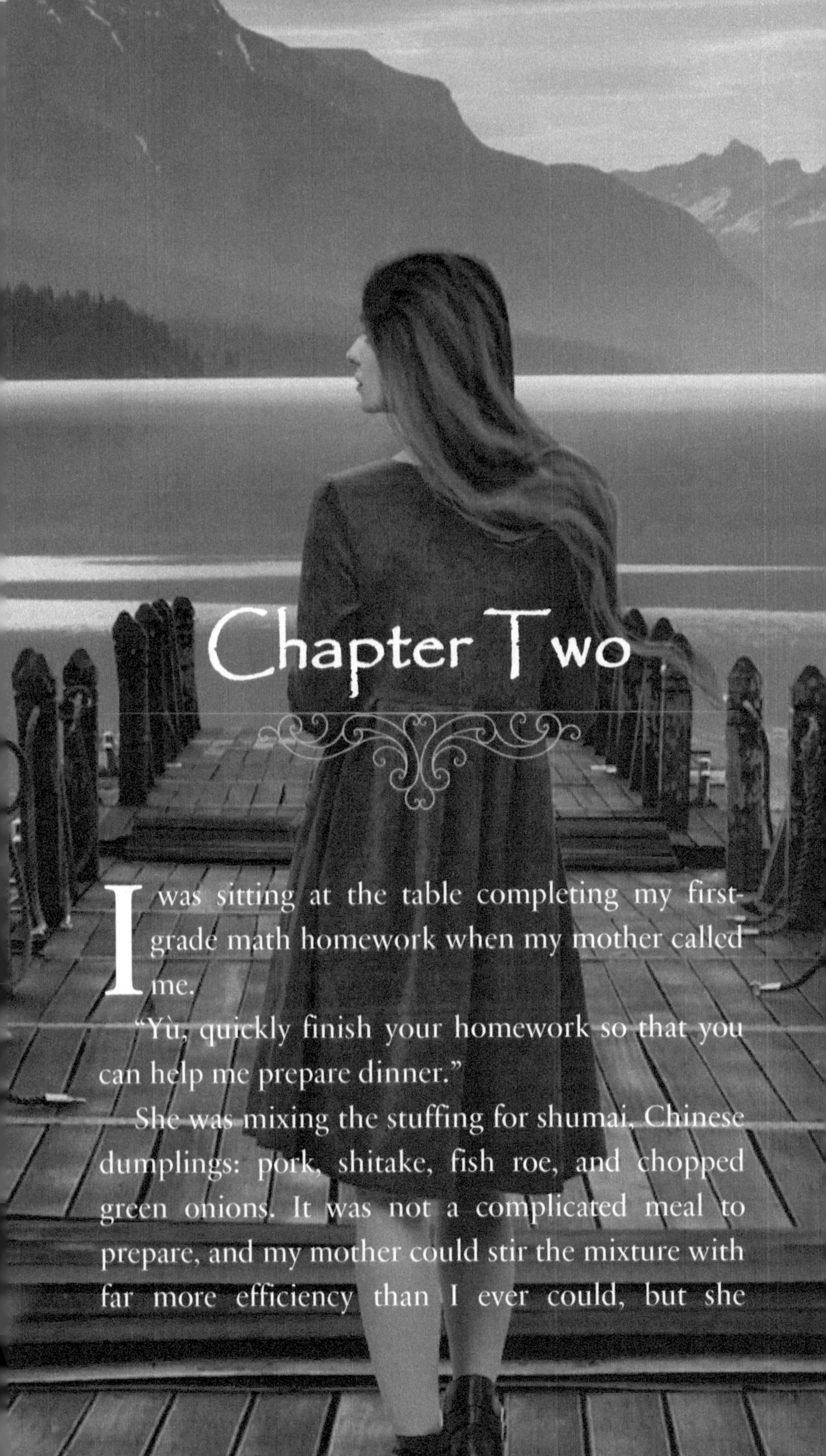

Chapter Two

I was sitting at the table completing my first-grade math homework when my mother called me.

"Yù, quickly finish your homework so that you can help me prepare dinner."

She was mixing the stuffing for shumai, Chinese dumplings: pork, shitake, fish roe, and chopped green onions. It was not a complicated meal to prepare, and my mother could stir the mixture with far more efficiency than I ever could, but she expected me to be the dream Chinese American daughter, known to everyone outside the family home as Jade Xiu.

I only had three more math questions to answer. I sucked on the tip of my pencil, tasting the metal tang of the lead, and the earthiness of the wood that made my tongue curl.

Whenever I closed my eyes and chewed my pencils, a habit my mother said was dirty as I would end up with a tree growing inside my belly, I pretended that I was in a forest, lying on the damp soil, branches making crisscrosses in the sunshine. Today, I kept my eyes open. The sound was turned down on the television because my father was reading the newspaper, and my mother was singing along to the Chinese station on the radio, but I could see the program that was about to start. *Saved by the Bell*.

My mom wanted me to learn to speak English at school, and Chinese at home. She wanted me to teach her to speak English, something she had managed to survive without since she came to America on a boat in 1965 with nothing more than a battered suitcase filled with clothes. How she survived was a miracle to me, looking back, but at the time, seven years old, I had already manipulated it to my advantage.

Saved by the Bell was about a group of kids in high school. It was shown on an American kids' channel, and because my mom didn't understand the language, I simply told her I was learning about school while also practicing my English. She had no reason to disbelieve me because I had always been a good girl. It would have been impossible to be anything else in this strict family unit.

I jumped as a wooden spoon rapped my knuckles. "Sorry, Ma," I said.

I hurriedly finished my homework, folded my exercise book, and stowed it neatly inside my backpack with my pencil and eraser.

"Here, mix this."

My mother handed me the bowl and wooden spoon, and I took over the stirring. We didn't speak much. My mother liked to be alone with her thoughts, which I guessed was why she still acted like she was living in Beijing. She would always compare my life to her life when she was a child, as though she wore her memories like a heavy cloak. It never made her happy, though.

Many times, I wanted to ask her why she always spoke about her childhood if it was so terrible; I mean, why did she not put it behind her and concentrate on her new life? But I never did because it would have been disrespectful.

"You not mixing it properly, Yù," she complained, yanking the bowl from my tiny soft-handed grasp. "My mother used to hit me whenever I did it wrong. You are lucky I not my mother."

I didn't remind her that she had already smacked me with the spoon for being slow.

"Yes, Ma," I said robotically.

"Remember what I told you." I groaned inwardly. This was how her lectures always began. "When your father bring me here on that rickety boat, it was hard for us. I am teaching you these skills so you will learn to appreciate everything that we do for you and Joseph."

Joseph is my brother. He is three years older than me. I will tell you a lot more about my brother in due course, and you will be able to make up your own mind about whether you think our parents treated us fairly and equally when we were growing up.

"I am grateful, Ma," I mumbled.

I was only seven, yet every day, I had to tell my parents how grateful I was to be their daughter; it was an exhausting habit that I feared I would never grow out of, and partly the reason why I was so enamored with TV shows on the kids' channels. Those children were respectful toward their parents and yet, I never once heard them say they were grateful for their life. I guessed it must be a Chinese thing.

"Then show it more," she snapped, raising the wooden spoon in the air as if to strike me. I flinched instinctively. Our eyes met briefly, and she lowered the spoon and resumed the stirring herself. "You must learn to be more appreciative," she continued, her voice lower so as not to disturb my father or Joseph, who was sprawled in an armchair, his legs swinging over the side, reading a comic. "China was in economic crisis when Pa and I came here. We had no money, and look at us now. We have house in city, and food on table."

"I appreciate it very much, Ma," I said. "I will learn how to cook Chinese dishes."

I watched her closely. My mother was relatively young for a woman who had endured so much hardship, but the distress and misery were already catching up with her, and she appeared older than she was. Her short black hair was cut perfectly straight above her shoulders, her cheekbones were high, and her stature short, a genetic trait she had unfortunately passed down to me.

We looked similar. I often saw myself in her when she was pressing our clothes, or scrubbing the oven, and I wondered if she thought the same when she looked at me.

"Set the table," said my mother, dismissing the conversation.

She cooked in silence, her hands seemingly everywhere. I watched her with one eye while keeping the other eye on the television screen. I couldn't lipread, but I was still able to follow the characters on the screen via their body language and their facial expressions. I smiled with them and frowned when something serious was happening. I studied the way they dressed, and the food they ate. And all the while, I was telling myself that when I went to high school, that would be me.

When the meal was ready, my mother pulled out chairs for Joseph and my father. We mostly ate in silence because my father didn't like mindless conversation. In all my childhood, I don't think he ever once asked me how I was doing in school. I didn't mind the silence — it was preferable to being ignored or lectured or ridiculed.

"Did you sign the permission slip for my school trip, Pa?" Joseph asked, chewing on a mouthful of shumai.

"Yes," said my dad, "but you must help Ma with chores as repayment."

Joseph nodded. While my parents were studying their food, he poked his tongue out at me so that I could see the lumps of dumpling clinging to it.

My father was a tall slim man with brown hair and a trimmed mustache, which sat perfectly above his lip. He wore a permanent serious expression. We never spoke the way fathers speak to their daughters in westernized movies, but I loved my father for the way he protected his family, despite the fact that I felt disconnected from him. I would often watch him from the kitchen window, with Joseph in the back yard, throwing the classic American football to each other.

I heard Joseph's laughter when my father dropped the ball, or my father's encouraging words, "That's it, son," or, "Well done, Joseph, great catch." I longed for the day that I would be invited to play with them, and my father would praise me for a great throw.

When we finished eating, my mother rose from the table and said, "No need to wash the dishes,

Joseph. Jade can take care of them." She smiled at him as he resumed his horizontal position draped across the armchair.

It never occurred to me to speak up about such things. I was already aware that their expectations and traditions were not to be questioned, and that I was expected to excel in everything. Chinese tradition was rooted in a history of profound misogyny. My mother told me how, in Beijing, families desperately hoped for sons at birth. The idea that a boy held more value to Chinese parents than a girl was a painful concept for me to grasp at such a young age, and I assumed that was the reason I was pushed to constantly achieve the highest grades at school, to master the language, whilst also learning to cook and keep the house clean like a good Chinese daughter. All so I could one day find a rich and successful man who would want me.

I did the dishes while patiently waiting for my chance to sit in front of the TV where I could pretend that I looked like the children on the screen.

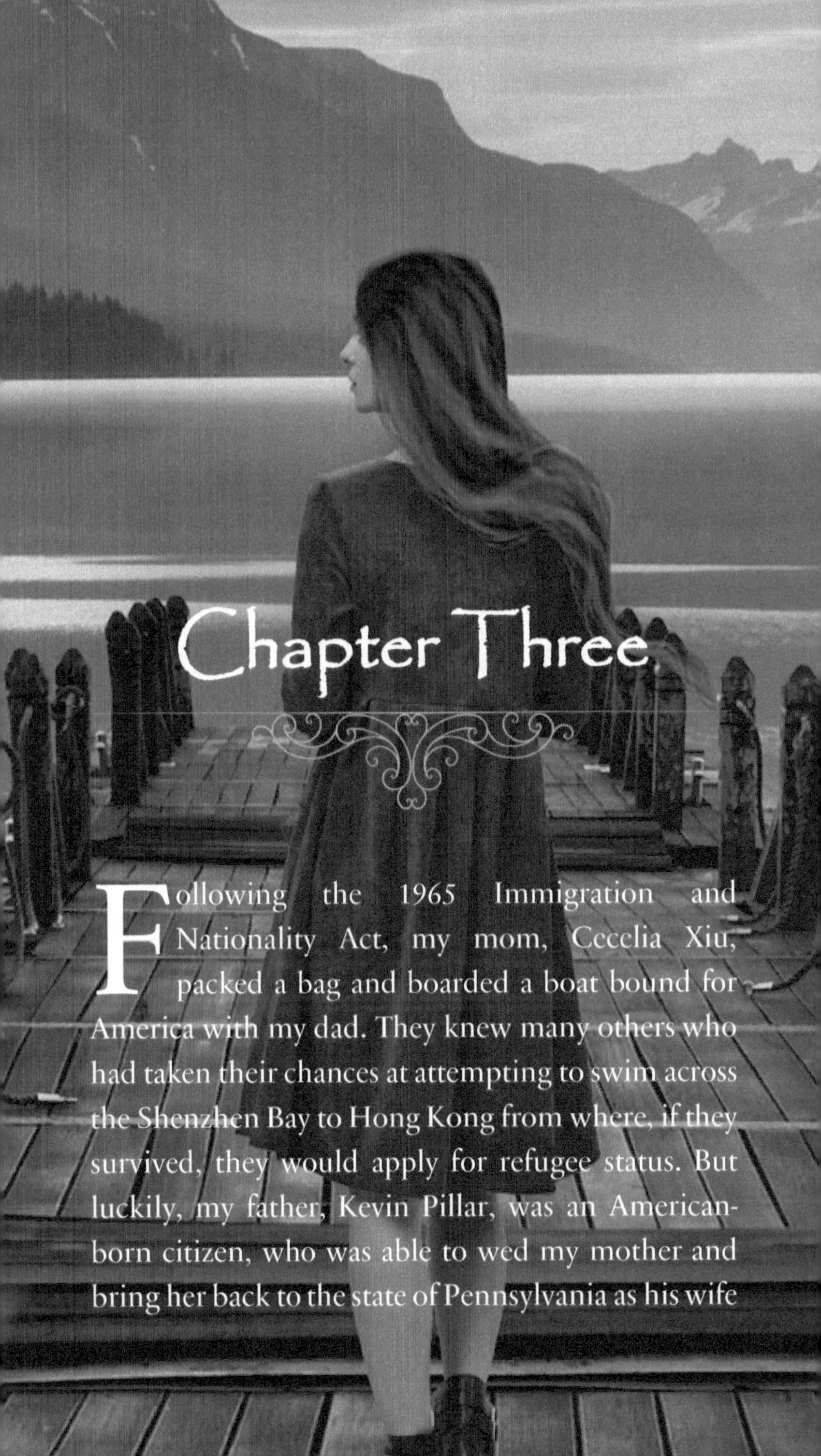

Chapter Three

Following the 1965 Immigration and Nationality Act, my mom, Cecelia Xiu, packed a bag and boarded a boat bound for America with my dad. They knew many others who had taken their chances at attempting to swim across the Shenzhen Bay to Hong Kong from where, if they survived, they would apply for refugee status. But luckily, my father, Kevin Pillar, was an American-born citizen, who was able to wed my mother and bring her back to the state of Pennsylvania as his wife before she eventually got her citizenship. But they weren't the only ones with the same mentality. Many other immigrants also did the same, all in attempts to free themselves from the corrupt government.

So, they all crammed into a tiny cabin with other fleeing Asians. They shared what little food they could afford, and Cecelia told my father stories of her dreadful childhood with her strict traditional grandparents who believed that children should work and study until they were permanently exhausted because they were expected to give something back.

She had heard about and imagined the blissful land of the free, where hardworking people could not possibly fail to succeed. It was the American dream, right? On arrival, they were spewed from the ship with their handheld luggage, the black and white photographs of my grandparents, starving bellies like shiny hardbacked beetles, and left to find their own way through the cracks.

She seized the first job opportunity that came her way. My father resumed his work in construction, building railroads and motorways, working long hours for little remuneration. My mother worked as a cleaner and a seamstress. The hours they worked never dwindled, and for many years, they worked six or seven days a week, rising early and finishing late. And when they had their first child, my mother convinced her husband to let them keep her maiden name, to carry on the unappreciated culture here in the states.

This new life did not come without its own problems. She did not speak the language, and my father was always too busy to help, and so communication, when it occurred, consisted of the few words she had managed to grasp, punctuated with much finger-pointing and sign language. Because of this, she was probably taken advantage of far more than she would have been had she been able to understand the basics of salary and worth.

The opportunity for her to advance by starting more professional careers simply never arose, and she never questioned it. I knew my mother had high hopes and dreams when she was a child, aspiring to be a pharmacist, but she gladly gave it up so she could give a better life to her kids, even if it meant sacrificing her own dream.

"I was grateful for my freedom," my mother often said.

It did not seem to me that working sixty-hour weeks was the kind of freedom I would aspire to, but

I believed her when she said it was easier than the life she had escaped from, from walking ten miles every day to school to surviving on nothing more than two bread rolls a day. It was a life I could never imagine living.

My mother spoke about foot-binding which, in ancient China, was said to be the way to become a desirable bride. Girls as young as five would have their feet massaged with oil, and all but their big toes broken and folded flat against the sole, before being bound tightly with silk. It was excruciating for the girls who were forced to walk on their broken toes, to break the arches of their feet to create the perfect tiny lotus shape, some as small as three inches.

My face must have reflected my horror at these tales for my mother used to remind me, "Respect your heritage, Yù."

This was quite difficult when my heritage was based on blatant sexism and the restriction of basic human rights. Men were encouraged to produce sons. Women were disappointed when they gave birth to daughters. Nevertheless, I listened and learned, and wanted nothing more than to be the perfect Chinese daughter.

We celebrated Chinese New Year with traditional food, music, and relaxation time as my parents were not inclined to be sociable. We celebrated the Lantern Festival and the Dragon Boat Festival. My mother religiously practiced and followed the Chinese horoscope.

And when I was alone in the house, which happened frequently with my parents' long working hours, I listened to Michael Jackson, Madonna, and Whitney Houston, and I pretended that I might one day become a famous singer who wore sparkly outfits and danced the moonwalk on a stage.

Chapter Four

My years at elementary school progressed in the same way as my first day. The classrooms changed, the lessons became more complicated and demanding, but I always sat in a seat at the back of the class, near the window, alone, where I didn't have to feel eyes boring holes into the back of my skull.

When my mother picked me up outside the school gates on my first day, she asked me how my day was, and I replied, "Good, Ma."

We walked home with hurried feet as though the ground had been scorched by the midday sun. She didn't make eye contact with the other mothers, or greet them with a wave and a, "Hi, there," so it was hardly surprising that the other girls treated me the same way.

That evening, during dinner, she asked me again in front of my father how my first day had been. There were frown lines across her forehead, and her lips were pursed while she awaited my response, and no one seemed to notice apart from me. I wondered if this was because she had been forced to ask me a second time for my father's benefit, and I felt like saying that Dad could have asked me himself, but that would have been disrespectful and would have earned me an early night with no dinner.

"It was good, Ma," I repeated.

I chewed the stir-fry that I had helped to prepare and kept my eyes on my plate. I wondered what they would say if I told them how the other girls had whispered behind their hands, giggling, pointing, and turning their nose up at the contents of my lunchbox. I wanted to ask Joseph if the boys in his Catholic school treated him the same way. But instead, I kept chewing until my throat grew so dry, I was afraid I would not be able to swallow my food.

"Were your classes easy?" asked my father.

He always ate from a bowl held close to his chin, the chopsticks moving deftly between his fingers, scooping the food into his mouth rather than raising it to his lips.

"Yes, Pa."

"Did they teach you to speak English?"

I glanced at Joseph, who didn't even seem to be following the conversation. I had never heard my parents ask Joseph if he had learnt to speak English. I had never seen Joseph sit on the yard with our mother and point to the sky, the grass, the flowers, and teach her all the English words.

Did my father expect me to become fluent overnight?

"I—I cannot learn to speak fluently in one day at school," I said.

"Jade Xiu!" My mother's chopsticks stung the back of my hand before I even realized that she had moved. "Answer the question with respect."

"Sorry, Ma." I kept my eyes on my food so that they would not see the tears welling in them. "Today, we learned about nouns and verbs and descriptive words."

"Kids' stuff," said Joseph. "Wait until you have to write essays about what you did on the weekend, and your dreams, and people you admire most in the world."

My father did not question Joseph about his essays. He lectured me on the need for a good education, and how I should pay particular attention in science class if I wanted to grow up to follow a career as a pharmacist.

I didn't ever remember telling my parents that I wanted to be a pharmacist. I didn't even know what a pharmacist was, but I guessed it might have had to do with my mom trying to pass her dream off onto me. Whatever the reason, it sounded a million miles from the shiny popstars I listened to on the radio when my parents were at work, and the actors I saw on TV, with their toothy white grins and their golden hair.

That night, I went to bed with an ache in my chest that would not go away even when I lied on my stomach with my fists rammed against my ribs. The one question my parents had not thought to ask me was: Did you make any friends? They were not interested in friends. Friends did not achieve good grades for you; they did not get you a boring career that earned lots of money; they did not earn you your graduation. And education was all my parents cared about.

But trying to fill the hole in my heart that night after my first day at school, I realized that making friends was the most important thing in the world to me because it was the only thing that would make me feel like I belonged.

I grew a little over the next couple of years, not much, and I remained the shortest girl in my year. But I outgrew my school uniform, which meant that my mother had to remind me constantly during the semester of the year I turned ten, how hard she had worked to buy me new skirts that reached my knees, and shirts that did not gape across my bosoms.

I worked hard at my studies. My grades were the highest in my class, and my teacher asked me how I would feel about skipping ahead to the next year; he felt that it would be good for me to be challenged by more difficult work aimed at children who were a year older than me. My chest swelled with pride that my teacher, who was almost as nice to me as Mr. Matthews had been when I started school, thought that I was bright enough to move up a grade.

I saw the way the other girls rolled their eyes whenever our marked test papers were handed back, and I had another A. I had heard Eliza Moon telling the others in the playground that she had seen me cheating in math class, copying Sarah Wright's work from over her shoulder. I had wanted to shout at them that if I had the highest score from cheating, then surely Sarah Wright would have had the highest score, too. But I didn't. It wouldn't have achieved anything anyway.

Mr. Boyd said that he would write a letter to my parents about moving up a grade, and that he would let me know when it was ready for me to collect it from the school office.

That evening, over dinner, I waited for my mother to ask me how my classes had been.

She seemed different tonight, as though a switch had been flicked on behind her eyes, lighting her up from the inside. "Joseph has some news," she said.

Our father stopped eating and set his bowl on the table in front of him.

"I've been chosen for the school football team," said Joseph, without waiting to be asked.

By now, Joseph was in high school, and he often came home late because he had football practice, or basketball practice, or a science project to complete in the school lab. All of this was allowed because he had no chores to do at home; I did all the chores after

I completed my homework and started preparing the evening meal.

"Do you hear that?" said our father to no one in particular. "Our son is on the football team." And then he carried on eating.

It was enough for Joseph, who appeared to have grown six inches. Even our mother was smiling, as though she could finally relax because her work was done. The lines smoothed out across her forehead, and her cheeks glowed.

They didn't ask how my day had been at school, and I didn't tell them about my conversation with Mr. Boyd.

When the dishes were done, I announced that I was going to bed because I had a headache. I brushed my teeth, changed into clean pajamas, which barely reached my ankles and wrists because I had been wearing them since I was seven, and pulled the duvet over my head. I was too hot, but I forced myself to pretend that I was on a Miami beach. I imagined the sunshine on my face making my scalp tingle, the warm sand beneath my toes, and the sound of the foamy ocean shushing against the shore. I stayed this way, motionless, until I fell asleep.

I woke early the following morning with stomach cramps. I kicked the duvet off me and lied curled like a snail, with my knees raised to my chin, and my arms wrapped around my shins to try and stop the pain from flaring. Pain after pain twisted my stomach. I wondered if this was how it felt to be poisoned because I was certain I was going to die. Then I realized that my pants were wet.

I was mortified. If I had peed myself without realizing and ruined the mattress, my mother would never let me forget how hard she had worked to provide me with a comfortable bed and clean clothes.

I waited for the burning ache in my stomach to subside a little, and then I swung my legs over the side of the bed and ran to the bathroom. It was worse than I had thought. I was bleeding. Each time I placed a tissue in between my legs, it came away bright crimson. Tears streamed down my cheeks. I was too young to die. I had not yet discovered what it felt like to be an all-American girl, play volleyball on the beach, go to college, and dance at parties.

All these things flashed before my eyes as I stared at the blood. I was not thinking about how badly I was hurting; I was mourning the loss of a bright sparkly fun-filled future I had only seen on a TV screen.

I heard my mother in the kitchen humming along to Chinese music and cooking noodles in the wok. I flushed the bloody tissue in the toilet and walked along the hallway to the kitchen. She had her back to me when I entered, so I stood there sniffling and whispered, "Ma." She must not have heard me because she didn't turn around.

"Ma!" I said louder.

When she finally looked at me, her face paled, and she moved the wok from the heat. "Are you sick?" she asked from a distance.

I nodded. "I think I have been poisoned."

She blinked at me, confused. "Who would have poisoned you? I always tell you to only eat food from this kitchen."

"I do, Ma," I said, clutching my stomach as more pain wrenched it from the inside. "I'm bleeding."

She glanced down at my pajama bottoms, realization spreading across her face. She replaced the wok over the hob and gave it a violent shake.

"Go to the bathroom. In the cabinet under the sink, you will find some pads. It will stop your pants from getting ruined."

That was it. She offered me no comfort for the pain in my stomach; she didn't tell me not to worry because the bleeding would not kill me. I wandered back along the hallway to the bathroom, found the pads, and inserted one into a fresh pair of pants. When I was dressed in my school uniform, I sat in the kitchen and waited for my breakfast. I ate in silence as usual, while my mother prepared my lunchbox, and then I walked to school, my own news about moving up a grade forgotten in my overwhelming wretchedness at what was happening to my body.

Chapter Five

I barely raised my head in math class that morning. I was uncomfortable. Everything about me felt wrong as though I had woken up in an alien body and had no idea who I was. The cramps in my stomach eased off gradually, but I was left feeling achy and sore, and frightened because the bleeding had not stopped. I felt as though, if it didn't stop soon, I would wake up the following morning shriveled like wilted spinach.

During my lunch break, I snuck into one of the rooms adjoining the cafeteria and opened my lunchbox. My mother had given me my favorite fried noodles and steamed rice with peas and chicken, and tears stung my eyes. I swiped the tears away with the back of my hand as a girl I didn't recognize approached me, carrying a lunchbox and sipping a carton of orange juice through a straw.

"Can I sit with you?" she asked. "I'm Jen."

"Sure," I nodded.

In two years, Jen was the only girl to have ever approached me like this, friendly and kind. She was the only girl to have spoken to me outside of class, and more tears welled in the corners of my eyes.

"I'm Jade." I sniffed and blinked and swallowed. "Are you new here?"

She grinned, and I noticed how clear her blue eyes were, like the sky on a sunny day. "It's my first day. I'm not very good at making friends."

I think I gasped then, and quickly raised a tissue to my mouth and faked a cough to hide my rudeness. Jen was so beautiful. Her blonde hair reached down to her waist, she had long dark eyelashes, and even her uniform looked different on her than it did on me. And still, she was admitting that she found it difficult to make friends. I didn't understand why; she was everyone's dream friend.

"Neither am I," I said.

"What do you have in your lunchbox?" she asked, peering at my noodles and rice.

"It's Chinese food," I said, trying to slide it out of her vision.

"Can I try it?"

I wondered if the other girls had sent her to ask as a dare, a kind of initiation into the friend group, but there was no one else in the room, and no one peering around the door, either.

"Sure." I shrugged. "If you want to."

She unwrapped the brown paper from around a sandwich cut into four tiny triangles with the crusts removed. "I'll swap you. A peanut butter and jelly quarter for some Chinese food."

I grinned at her, and I realized it was the first time I had smiled at anyone in school since the day I started. I had always wanted to try a peanut butter and jelly sandwich, and it was everything I had dreamt it would be: crunchy, sweet, and… normal. And Jen's eyes widened as I scooped up some noodles and rice on my chopsticks.

"Oh my god, I can't wait to tell my mom about this," she said with a mouthful of spicy food.

"I can teach you how to make it one day," I said. "If you like."

We talked about teachers, our classes, and TV shows while we ate our lunch together. I told her that English was my favorite subject, and that I was still learning to speak the language fluently. I was not so keen on math because sometimes the numbers didn't make sense to me even when the teacher explained it step-by-step, but then there were moments when it was like someone had switched a light on in my book, and I could suddenly understand it.

Jen laughed. "You're funny, Jade. And you don't speak any different to how I speak."

I was taken aback. I guessed I was so consumed by the other girls treating me as though I were different, and by speaking English in school and Chinese at home, that I had not taken a moment to stand back and truly listen to myself. It was the first time also that I allowed myself to think that, one day, I might belong here.

That afternoon, Jen was in the same music class as me, followed by English with Mr. Boyd. When the bell sounded for the end of school, he asked me to stay behind. I waved goodbye to Jen and told her I would see her in the morning.

Mr. Boyd held up a letter for me inside a crisp official-looking white envelope; my parents' names were written on the front in neat blue ink. "This is the note to your parents about you moving up a grade, Jade." The teacher smiled. "Did you speak to them?"

I had forgotten all about Mr. Boyd's suggestion that I move up to the next class. I could still smell Jen's shampoo. I felt her absence beside me as though we had been born twins, and I imagined how it would be if I were suddenly snatched away from her now when we had only just found each other.

I was still feeling emotional because of the bleeding I had discovered that morning, and the uncertainty that I might be dying, and I knew that I couldn't change classes. Not now.

I nodded. "They did not seem too keen on the idea," I lied. I swallowed and kept my eyes focused on his mouth so that I didn't have to make eye contact. "I think… I think they are worried about me not fitting in."

Tears welled uncontrollably, and I allowed them to trickle down my cheeks. Mr. Boyd took a tissue from the box on his desk and handed it to me. He nodded without smiling. It was the first time I had ever lied to anyone, and I was consumed by guilt and anxiety, my blood rushing around my veins and almost drowning my thoughts. But at the same time, I felt elated. I had finally taken control of my own life because I had a friend, and I was not about to lose her.

I had a fleeting moment of panic that Mr. Boyd would speak to my parents about it and tell them he was quite disappointed that they were holding me back, but then I told myself, they never attended teacher-parent sessions, and my mother's English still wasn't great so she would need me to translate anything he said to her. It was a devious way of thinking, and quite unnatural to me.

But I was desperate. While what I had said to him was a lie, it was what I wanted my parents to say. If I could conjure the perfect parents with a magic wand, I would want them to care about me fitting in rather than getting the best grades.

"I understand," said Mr. Boyd. "But you are well-liked, Jade. I wish they would reconsider because it would be beneficial to you in the long run." He gave me the envelope. "Please ask them to read it, and let me know their decision next week. Maybe they will change their mind."

I hid the envelope in the bottom of my backpack, and I never showed it to my parents.

Chapter Six

My parents never knew about Jen. They never asked about anything other than grades and teaching them new English words, and I never offered them any information. At home, I was still the good little Chinese daughter — and I mean that literally as I still had not reached five feet — and in school, I was Jade Xiu, Jen's best friend.

I rarely saw Joseph as he was always attending after-school activities and football practice, and on weekends, he was either training or playing for the school team. Our parents never mentioned Joseph's grades, homework, or tests; they simply assumed that he was doing the best that he could without the need for them to constantly push him.

So, when Jen asked me to go to her house after school one Friday and stay for dinner, I said yes. It was only afterwards that I considered how I was going to make this happen.

That evening, when we were eating our evening meal, which had become later and later with the increasing number of hours worked by my father, I waited for them to ask me about school. I kept my eyes on my food, my arms close to my sides and making myself as small and inconspicuous as possible, and said, "I'm staying behind after school on Friday for extra English tutoring."

My father peered at me from beneath lowered eyebrows. "Why extra tutoring?" he growled. "Why are you behind?"

"I'm not behind, Pa," I said in my brightest voice. "They are giving extra classes for anyone who wants to work harder. It will mean getting into a better class when I go to high school." I deliberately used all the words that I knew would impress them, all the words that mattered. Work harder. Better class.

My father nodded and continued eating. That was his approval. It was also a signal for my mother to speak about school in Beijing. "In China, children started school after breakfast and stayed until lunch. We went home for lunch and a nap, and then went back to school until dinner, and then we went back to school in the evening until it was time to go to bed."

I had heard these stories before but had never really paid much attention to them. Now, I listened to them and wondered why Chinese children were allowed no freedom outside of their studies.

"We had music lessons during weekends," continued my mother. "And any other lessons, there was no time for during the week. This is no hardship staying behind after school on Friday."

"No, Ma," I said. "I know we are lucky."

By the age of ten, I had become adept at saying what my parents wanted to hear. It was only the second time I had told a lie, and this time, I did not feel the slightest pang of guilt.

Jen's house was like many other houses I saw on American TV shows. In size, it might not have been any different from our house, but it was like walking into a foreign world or a movie studio. The kitchen was pale and pretty with warm pine cupboards and floral curtains framing the windows. The walls were white with pictures of red and white spotted teacups and teapots all over them; the accessories were all red and white too, like a diner or a malt shop. The window was open, and I could hear birds singing on the trees in their back yard, and Jen's mom was baking cookies. She removed a tray from the oven and slid steaming chocolate chip cookies onto a red and white plate for us to eat while she filled tall tumblers with creamy milk.

"My favorites," said Jen, clapping her hands and helping herself to a large cookie.

Her mom slid a smaller plate in front of her to hold the biscuit, which was still too hot to handle.

"Do you like cookies, Jade?" her mom asked me.

Jen's mom was Jen with a few lines around her eyes when she smiled. If someone had asked me to draw how I pictured my friend to look in thirty years, I would have drawn her mom, Josephine.

"Yes, thank you," I said.

I couldn't tell her that I had never tasted a cookie before, that my parents only brought Asian food into the house because they believed that was the highest-quality cuisine. Sweets were never allowed. Junk food, a sin.

"Oh, so polite, honey." Josephine fondled my hair and tucked it around my shoulders. She leaned forward and cupped my cheeks between her hands. "So pretty. No wonder my Jen is always talking about you."

I glanced at Jen, and she shrugged. "You're the prettiest girl in school, and everyone knows it. That's why they don't want to be friends with you. They're jealous."

"Take no notice of them, Jade," said Josephine. "Girls will always be like that when they feel threatened, and trust me, it will only get worse in high school. You will always know which girls are genuine by the way they handle your beauty." She kissed Jen on the top of her head. "But I guess your mom has already given you this advice."

I stuffed a large chunk of cookie into my mouth and waited for it to cool down before I chewed. I was storing this conversation up in my head so that I could think about it later in the privacy of my own room. I couldn't recall a time when my mom had ever touched my hair and told me that I was pretty, or had ever given me any advice other than *Don't bother with friends because they drag you down*, and I guess it was a lot to process.

Jen's room was a room fit for a princess. Literally. She had a canopy above her bed, covered with a pink veil that draped around the headboard so that it was like sleeping inside a fluffy pink cloud. She had pink and gold sequined cushions, and shelves lined with glass ornaments in every color imaginable. She had a doll's house in one corner that reached to my waist, and inside, the rooms were decorated with wallpaper and curtains, and the bedroom had a canopy that matched Jen's. It was magical. I was in love with Jen's house.

I knew I shouldn't have, but I sat on Jen's bed, staring, staring at her dolls, her vanity, and her princess canopy, comparing it to my room. My room was smaller, sure, but it wasn't that tearing a hole in my chest; it was that my room was so bleak compared to this airy pink room where Jen slept every night. My walls were a grubby color with no name. My bed was pushed into a corner with no headboard and no fancy cushions. I had a desk and a functional dresser where all my clothes were folded into neat piles, but there were no ornaments, no dolls, no pretty, silver hairbrush and sparkly clips for my hair. If you took a picture of each of our rooms, they could have been used in class to describe light and dark. Day and night. Happy and sad.

Jen had a little sister, Emily, who ran in and out with Barbie dolls for us to dress. "Sorry," said Jen. "Em is being a nuisance, but it's only because she likes you. If she didn't like you, she wouldn't keep coming in."

I smiled. "It's okay. I like dressing her dolls." I was too embarrassed to tell her that I didn't have any dolls of my own.

Jen had posters on her baby pink walls. Michael Jackson. Gloria Estefan. Sandy and Danny from *Grease*. She had postcards pinned to the wall from other parts of America, a picture of a rainbow painted in kindergarten by Emily, a black and white photograph of a man and a woman in clothes that were from a long time ago. Jen's grandparents.

I pointed to the poster from *Grease*. "Is that a movie?" I asked.

She widened her eyes at me. "Don't tell me you've never seen *Grease*!"

I shook my head, suddenly embarrassed. "Come with me." Jen took my hand and led me back into the living room where her parents were watching TV. "Mom, can we watch *Grease*, please? Jade has never seen it."

Josephine smiled at us; her parents were always smiling. "Sure, honey, you know where the tape is. I think Jen has watched this video more times than the rest of us put together," she said to me. "You're in for a real treat."

We watched the movie while Jen's mom prepared dinner. I could not take my eyes off the TV screen. I thought that Sandy and Danny were the most beautiful people I had ever seen, and in my head, it was how I pictured myself in high school, meeting a boy in a black leather jacket and being part of a gang like the Pink Ladies.

Jen sang along to all the songs, and when it came to *Summer Nights*, she kept pausing the video and teaching me the lyrics. By the time dinner was served, I knew them word for word, and Jen and I were standing on the sofa, pretending to sing into our fists as though they were microphones.

We sat at the kitchen table, breathless and pink-cheeked. "You girls are natural talents," said Josephine. "You should start a rock band when you're older."

I thought that Jen would tell her mom to stop being silly, but she grinned at me and offered me her pinkie beneath the table where we made a silent pact to become famous rock stars one day.

We ate meatloaf and homemade coleslaw, washed down with soda that Jen's dad made from a soda machine. It was the happiest day of my life.

I wished I had someone to talk to about Jen and our rock star pact, but my parents would have stopped our friendship somehow if they had known about it, and I knew that I had to keep the Jade I was with Jen entirely separate from the Yù I was at home.

That evening, before I let myself into the house, I pressed my cheeks down into their normal expression, thought of all the chores my mother would still expect me to help out with so that all traces of my smile were erased, and locked the song lyrics away in a special place in my heart.

My mother was in the kitchen when I walked in. My mother was always in the kitchen when she wasn't working; it was as though she lived in the room, preparing food, chopping, slicing, frying. I had always thought it was how mothers lived, but now that I had seen Josephine baking cookies and with her legs tucked beneath her on the sofa while she drank coffee, I realized just how different my family was compared to other families.

"I saved you noodles," said my mother from over her shoulder.

I couldn't even look at her in case she spotted the glimmer in my eyes. "I'm not hungry," I said, keeping my backpack over my shoulders.

"How were your extra studies?"

"Good, Ma."

I went to my room and curled on my bed, pretending that I had a princess canopy above my head.

Chapter Seven

My parents sent me to a Catholic High School; it was a natural progression from elementary school. Roman High was not nearly as strict as Redeemer and didn't require the students to wear uniform. It was the first real freedom I had ever experienced with the way I looked, and I spent many hours in Jen's bedroom discussing clothes, hairstyles, and growing up.

Jen's mom took her to the mall and bought her clothes during the holidays before we started high school. My parents still worked long hours, and I spent all my time with Jen, rising early to begin my chores before I left home, and returning before my parents finished work to complete the tasks.

I rarely saw Joseph as he woke up late in the mornings and generally after I was out of the house, and his evenings were spent either in his bedroom or at football practice. There was a part of me that missed my brother's company, but I was too wrapped up in Jen to dwell on it. I had become a pro at compartmentalizing the various aspects of my life and storing them in secret rooms in my mind.

"Is your mom taking you shopping for new clothes?" Josephine asked one summer day.

Jen had never been to my house or met my parents, and I dreaded the day she would find out how we lived as though we were still in China, despite my mom's desperation to leave her home country and start a new life here.

"No… I don't know," I mumbled. "We haven't really spoken about it."

I saw Josephine staring at the jeans I was wearing, which were too short for me and had worn holes in the knees, and my T-shirt, which barely reached the waistband of my denims. She was too nice to comment on it, but I knew she would remember that she rarely saw me wearing anything else.

I knew I had to broach the subject with my mother, so that evening, I prepared a special meal of fried chicken noodles with steamed vegetables and mushrooms in soy sauce before she came home. I had picked some daisies from the park on my way back, stuck them in a clean jar, and placed them on the windowsill. My mother didn't even notice when she came in.

"Where's your brother?" she asked, serving the meal into bowls without even removing her shoes.

"In his room, Ma," I said.

"Call him."

We rarely waited for my father these days. He ate alone in front of the TV when he finished work. After, he would drink glasses and glasses of whiskey, his eyes glucd to the screen, his mouth a tiny button beneath his mustache. The only person he made conversation with was my mom.

Joseph emerged from his room like a snail peeping out from its shell, a smile forming on his lips the closer he got to the kitchen and food. He looked pale. I didn't know why I hadn't noticed this before, but I guessed I was so wrapped up in Jen and her family and trying to avoid drawing attention to myself, that it came as a bit of a shock. He passed me as he took his seat, and I was certain I could smell cigarette smoke. I gasped, and he glared at me. He must have realized why I had reacted because he gave me an almost imperceptible shake of his head before he took his seat.

"Smells good, Ma," he said.

"Yù prepared dinner," she said, raising her eyes to me.

"Wow!" said my brother. "When did you learn to cook?"

At first, I thought he was joking, but he took a mouthful of mushrooms and closed his eyes, savoring the taste.

"I have always helped Ma," I said quietly.

My chest was swelling with pride that our mother had not claimed to have cooked the meal herself, and because it felt like the first time that we had made eye contact in years.

We ate in silence for several minutes, my stomach churning at the thought of asking Ma for new clothes. Eventually, I took a deep breath and blurted out, "Ma, can I have new clothes for high school?"

She stared at me mid-chew and placed her chopsticks across the bowl like a bridge. "What is wrong with the clothes you have?"

I dropped my eyes. "They are too small for me, Ma."

I wanted to tell her about Jen's new clothes, but as far as my parents were concerned, Jen didn't even exist.

My mother was silent. Even Joseph had stopped eating, his eyes on me, on my clothes. I could tell that he was thinking about the way I dressed; maybe he was even comparing me to the other girls in high school.

"I let them down," said our mother. She picked up her chopsticks and began eating again, conversation closed.

Tears stung my eyes. I didn't want my clothes to be let down. I wanted *new* clothes. It wasn't that I was jealous of Jen; I simply wanted to start high school as the new me. Jade, not Yù. Jade, the all-American girl who spoke like the other kids and dressed like the other kids, even if I looked different.

Joseph cleared his throat. "I think Jade's right," he said. "You don't want the other girls picking on her because she's wearing kids' clothes. You can't let down a pair of jeans that doesn't fit." He winked at me, and I swiped a tear from my cheek with the back of my hand before my mother noticed.

"They not care about clothes," said our mother. Her English had improved a lot, but she always spoke with a Chinese accent, unlike me and Joseph, who could have passed for native Americans. "I put up with far worse than this when I came to America."

"Then you'll understand how it feels," said Joseph calmly. It was the first time I had ever heard him speak back to our parents, and I didn't know what to say. "Don't make it any harder for Jade than it needs to be."

My mother stared at Joseph, her eyes dark like wet stones, and then she leaned forward and kissed his forehead. It was the only display of affection I had ever seen from her, and I could not stop staring. Joseph dropped his chopsticks, and then fussed over picking them up.

She sat back down and said to me, "I make you clothes."

It was not exactly what I wanted, but it was better than nothing.

When we finished, and our mother was clearing away the dishes, I mouthed behind her back a *thank you* to Joseph.

He shrugged, and whispered, "I tried."

My mother had a sewing machine which she kept in a corner of the living room so that when she was using it, she was facing the wall with her back to the rest of us, the sound humming above the voices on the TV. She made her own clothes, which was fine because she didn't care how she looked when she left the house to go to work. I was worried that she would make the same clothes for me: black wide-legged trousers that swung above her ankles and white blouses with short sleeves.

My fears were realized when I woke one morning to find the handmade clothes folded neatly at the bottom of my bed. I kicked them onto the floor. I was not going to try them on, and I couldn't face seeing her before she went to work because I would have to force a grateful thank you, or she would be angry with me.

I told Jen later that day when we were sipping sodas in her back yard beneath a giant rainbow-colored umbrella, while Emily collected pretty pebbles and arranged them in clock-shaped patterns on the grass. Jen pursed her lips in thought and then said, "Jade, I have a heap of clothes that my mom wants to take to the thrift store. Why don't you take them?"

She looked scared, as though I might accuse her of treating me like a charity case, but I couldn't contain the smile that spread across my face. Jen's clothes were everything I had always wanted. But then I thought there was no way my mother would let me leave the house wearing someone else's clothes, garments that she would never have approved of, and certainly would never have bought for me.

My smile faded. "She will never let me wear them."

Jen nodded thoughtfully. "She won't see you in school though — they could be your secret school clothes."

We spent the rest of the day sorting through plastic bags filled with clothes that were a little too small for Jen, but fit me perfectly. I paraded around her bedroom like a catwalk model, and Jen even called her mom and Emily in to watch. Josephine clapped her hands and said, "You look gorgeous, honey," and I wished that she were my mom.

When I arrived home later that day with my bags of new clothes that still smelled of Jen, I closed my bedroom door and unfolded them one at a time, holding them against me and recalling the earlier fashion show of which I had been the star. I had never owned anything so pretty and sparkly and… American before, and I suddenly felt like I would explode with happiness. I folded them all as small as I could and layered them in the bottom of my dresser with my regular clothes on top. Doing the laundry was one of my chores so I wasn't concerned that my mother would find them unless she went rooting through my dresser, but she would only do that if she were suspicious. All I had to do was pretend that I loved the clothes she had made for me.

I was nervous when I went to bed the night before my first day of high school. Nervous and excited, too. With my dresser full of bright shiny clothes, I felt like I was going to bed as Yù and stepping out of the house the following morning as Jade Xiu, a regular American girl attending a regular American high school, with regular American friends. It sounds cliché now, but I truly believed that my first day at high school was going to be the first day of the rest of my life.

And I guess it was.

Chapter Eight

My mother left for work early as usual. She didn't even say that she hoped I had a good day at high school, and I wondered if she even remembered that it was my first day. Joseph left before me. I didn't ask where he was going or why he was leaving so early — I was just grateful to have the house to myself.

I had already chosen my outfit: a cute red poodle skirt with large white polka dots, and a white T-shirt with a picture of a slice of cherry pie on the front and the words CUTIE PIE. I winked at my reflection in the mirror and turned this way and that, posing as if I were one of the child actors I saw on TV. I already felt like Jade Xiu. I sounded like Jade Xiu. I had the best friend in the whole world, and I was in high school. I was so excited I could have screamed, but instead, I contented myself with giggling out loud.

Jen and I walked together, chatting and giggling as though we hadn't seen each other every day throughout the summer. It was strange seeing hordes of kids out of uniform, and even stranger going to a school with boys. It was as though we had suddenly been told that we were grown up enough to socialize with the opposite sex, and I felt a kind of power surging through my veins.

Not that I was interested in boys; I was only fourteen. It was simply because it meant that we were equals. After years of watching my brother receive privileges that I never had, I was attending a school where I would be in the same classes as boys, where the teachers would look at me and not regard me as inferior to the boy on my left.

If I thought Redeemer was huge, it was nothing compared to Roman. Everything was bigger, wider, longer. The corridors. The halls. The classrooms. There were kids everywhere, the conversations and laughter, louder and more boisterous. Boys pushed each other around playfully. Girls laughed, squealed, and hugged.

Jen and I waited in line at the reception, and I breathed it all in. I watched the other kids who took no notice of me. I had pinned my hair back on one side with a sparkly red clip — one of Jen's — and even that made me feel more special.

And then I heard a noise by the lockers, a clanging sound like a door being slammed, and I glanced up to see a boy pinned against the wall by an Asian kid. The Asian kid was shorter than the boy, but stockier, well-built, and he was not backing down, but had his face pushed right up into the boy's. My heart was racing. I could only guess that the boy pushed up against the wall had said something offensive and hadn't expected a reaction like this. And then the Asian kid dropped his arms and stepped away, glancing in our direction, and I realized that it was Joseph.

I averted my eyes. I felt my breath catching in my throat, and my blood rushing through my veins. It was as though my whole new world of high school that I had built up to be something wondrous, magical, and filled with music had dropped out from under my feet and transformed into something dark and difficult. It was just an extension of elementary school, and suddenly, I wished I was at home, safe in my bedroom.

"Do you know that boy?" Jen asked. "Jade? Are you okay?"

I considered lying and saying that I had no idea who he was. But Jen was my best friend, my only friend, and she would find out soon enough.

I nodded. "That's my brother."

Jen stared at the boy as he strode past us, fists clenched and chin held high, daring someone else to pick on him.

"That's Joseph?"

I had told her about Joseph, about how he didn't need to share the chores with me or regale our parents with stories about his impressive grades or teach them to speak English. I had told her how I thought he smoked cigarettes even though I had no idea where he was getting the money from. I had also told her how he had stood up to our mother when she wanted to let down my already too-small clothes.

"Whoa! He's cute," said Jen.

She squeezed my hand, but it didn't chase away the shadow that had fallen over my day.

Jen and I were in all the same classes apart from science, which was okay because I didn't enjoy science, something I had never confessed to my parents, who still expected me to be a pharmacist when I finished school; I intended to drop the subject as soon as I could. We stuck together as though our arms were smeared with glue.

At lunchtime, in the cafeteria, I used the coins I had saved up from doing extra chores around the house to buy a tuna mayo wrap and a carton of orange juice, though I was too anxious to enjoy the food. Everything was so surreal; it felt like stepping through a time warp and finding myself in another country, on another planet, in someone else's body.

Two girls came over to our table and asked Jen if they could join us. I didn't even care that they didn't ask me. They sat down with their trays of food and introduced themselves as Laura and Britany. They attended a different elementary school so neither of us knew the girls, but they seemed nice, and not put off by the fact that I was half-Asian.

"What classes do you have this afternoon?" asked Britany.

Jen checked her schedule and said that we had double music followed by double English.

"Have you seen Mr. Gentile, the music teacher? He's lush," said Laura.

"Lush?" I asked. This was a new word to me.

"Cute," Laura said. "I already have a serious crush."

Her cheeks grew hot and pink to prove it, and I smiled at her.

"Ooh, Jade, you'll be okay then," said Jen. She turned to the other girls. "Wait until you hear Jade sing."

I felt my own cheeks growing hot and blurted out, "We're going to be rock stars one day."

I felt silly as soon as the words were out there, but Britany and Laura smiled and said they wanted front row tickets to our first concert.

Laura was not wrong. Mr. Gentile *was* lush. When he walked into the classroom, I stared at him openmouthed until Jen nudged me with her elbow.

"This is my new favorite class," she whispered.

We spent the lesson learning instruments that we were not comfortable with, and I ended up with a violin, which I tried my hardest to avoid. My mother played violin; it was one of the many things she was forced to do as a child, which meant it was the last thing I wanted to do. When Mr. Gentile watched me for a couple of minutes and said that I was a natural, my cheeks grew hot for all the wrong reasons, and I had to look out the window until they cooled down.

The rest of the week passed without much going on. The four of us met for lunch every day and shared our food. Laura and Britany were fussy eaters, picking at plain chicken sandwiches, a banana or apple, and a yogurt. I wondered how my mother would have coped if Joseph or I were fussy eaters who refused to eat her cooking.

It was Friday when Laura suggested that the four of us meet at the diner on Saturday for milkshakes and burgers. It seemed that now that we were old enough to attend school without a uniform, it also meant that we could go to the diner without our parents. I guessed it was the start of us finding our independence and becoming young adults.

The others were all chatting about where they should meet and what they were going to wear.

"You'll come, Jade?" asked Jen.

I had never been inside a diner. Sure, I had seen them on TV, mesmerized by the colors, the booths, the imaginary aromas of burgers and hot dogs and fries, servers on roller skates and wearing frilly white aprons tied around their waists, but I had never stood outside a real-life diner and imagined how it would feel to step through the doors. But it wasn't fear of the unknown that made me hesitate. It was money.

My mother had only recently started offering me pocket money during the summer, and I was saving all the change she gave me to buy food from the school cafeteria. It didn't leave me with any money to spend during the weekends. And Jen's birthday was coming up soon, and I wanted to get her the record that she kept talking about as I knew her mom was going to give Jen her very own record player.

It made my head spin trying to work it all out, so I smiled at her and said, "Sure, can't wait!"

Jen and I arranged to walk into town together and meet Laura and Britany there. I should have been excited about my first ever milkshake in a diner with my new friends, but my excitement was outweighed by the very real, very dark fear that I would have no money to pay for it.

Friday afternoon came and went, and I could not remember having learned anything in any of my classes. Walking home, Jen talked about the homework set by our English teacher, and her grandma coming to visit on Sunday, and how she liked Britany's new shoes. I must have nodded and answered in all the right places because she didn't stop until I waved goodbye when she reached her street.

When I let myself into the house, I went straight to my room and flopped onto my bed. I considered not going tomorrow. I could tell Jen that I wasn't feeling well, or that I had been sick or had a headache. She would understand. She wouldn't judge me for backing out, either. But the thing that was making tears sting behind my eyes was knowing that they would go without me, and they would have fun, leaving me out of the loop. They probably wouldn't even miss me. It was so unfair. Why should I not get to have fun, too?

I knew I had to go; I just needed to find some money.

I was in the kitchen frying vegetables in the wok when my mother came home from work. Because I had grown a little, we were now the same height, only she appeared smaller because of the way she held herself. I had never really noticed it before, but she kind of curled in on herself, as though she were hiding or embarrassed to be here, whereas I was straight-backed, head held high the way my friends and peers carried themselves. I was already more American than my mother would ever be.

She came into the room, slid a woven cloth bag over the back of a kitchen chair, and tossed her clasp-purse into one of the kitchen drawers. The routine took me by surprise. Until now, I had always been so busy avoiding my mother that I had paid no attention to her actions. Heat flared in my cheeks at my next thought. I knew where her purse was.

My mother leaned over the wok, breathed in, and added some more chilies. Without speaking, she left the room and went to change out of her work clothes and into something comfortable, which meant the same style clothes she wore during the day, only cleaner. I didn't hesitate. There was no one else in the house, and I knew she would only be a couple of minutes, so I opened the drawer and looked inside her purse. There were lots of folded notes and a few coins. I quickly snapped the purse shut, slipped it back inside the drawer, and closed it. I was stirring the vegetables when she returned.

"How was school?" she asked.

"Good, Ma," I said.

I could have just asked her if she would give me some money to go to the diner with my new friends, but I already knew what the answer would be: "You don't need friends, Yù. Why you need to go diner when there is food here?"

I was filled with shame. Shame that my friends were more important to me than my own mother. Shame that I was contemplating taking some of the money she worked so hard for. I finished preparing dinner in silence, hoping that she would not hear my angry heart or see the shame on my face.

After dinner, I lied on my bed with my face buried in my pillow. I only wanted a couple of dollars. I didn't think that was too much to ask.

The first time was the hardest. I barely spoke at the diner; Jen, Laura, and Britany were all so loud that it didn't matter whether I was quiet, burying myself in guilt and shame. They spoke enough for them to not miss my voice.

My guilt was exacerbated further by the fact that I loved the experience. I loved eating a cheeseburger smothered in ketchup and salty fries. I loved the frothy creamy chocolate milkshake. I loved being with my friends. It gave me a sense of belonging that eventually outweighed the guilt of stealing from my mother's purse, and I convinced myself that if they were normal parents, I wouldn't have had to stoop to such drastic measures.

The other girls had money. They were comfortable with seeing their friends outside of school because they didn't have to lie about where they had been or who they spoke to. A couple of boys greeted us when they came in, and the girls waved and smiled at them while I kept my head down so they wouldn't notice me.

It was the first time I took money from my mother without asking, and it was the first time I felt resentment forming a knot deep inside my chest like an angry messy ball of yarn that would eventually pull so tight, I would forget how to unravel it.

Chapter Nine

The first year of high school passed in a flash. There was always so much going on: sports, drama club, art exhibitions, homework, extra study periods. The girls didn't meet up every weekend, but we spent a lot of time together at the park, sitting under the shade of the trees while we did our homework. Britany had a radio that she always brought along; we took turns standing up and singing in front of each other as though the park were our stage.

Mr. Gentile remained my favorite teacher — he was everyone's favorite teacher. He started a choir group which we all joined. I made the mistake of telling my mother about it one night over dinner.

She shook her head before I had even finished the sentence. "No choir group," she said. "You study, not sing."

"But, Ma," I began.

Her chair scraped backwards across the kitchen floor. She picked up her half-eaten bowl of noodles, steamed rice, and vegetables, and tossed it into the sink without scraping the food away first.

As she left the room, she muttered in Chinese, "You would not speak to me like this if we were in Beijing."

I glanced at Joseph, who watched her back as she walked away. He shrugged.

"I like singing," I said. "It doesn't interfere with my studying. Why won't she listen?"

He shook his head. "She doesn't want us to grow up and have to do the jobs they do. In her head, if you get good grades, you'll get a decent job and be comfortable."

I almost told him that he sounded just like her, but instead, I said, "I could get a good job as a singer.

I could be famous and live in a mansion in LA. Doesn't she think of that?"

"Forget it, Jade," said Joseph. "That's never going to happen."

Because my mother never gave me a chance to explain, or ever asked about my singing, I was more determined than ever to take part in every singing opportunity that arose. I sang at the Christmas Carol Concert at the school ball, which was rammed with parents who had come to listen, plenty with tears in their eyes.

When I was singing, I forgot that I was Chinese American. I forgot that my parents sailed here on a boat from Beijing. I was just Jade Xiu, a fourteen-year-old American girl who couldn't wait to be famous.

So, when Mr. Gentile announced that he was arranging an ambitious production of the musical *West Side Story* for the lower years, I put my name down to audition. He spoke to me in music class and said that he was happy I wanted to audition, which made me glow inside. Jen nudged me in the ribs with her elbow and whispered, "He would be crazy not to give you a part."

I wasn't even nervous at the audition, which took place during lunchbreak the week before Christmas.

Mr. Gentile had been teaching us one of the songs from the show, and that was what he asked everyone to perform while he watched with a couple of the seniors who had starred in the previous year's summer production of *Carousel*. The cast was not being announced until school reopened in January, and I spent my Christmas break, while my parents worked, chatting with the girls about it non-stop. They were all convinced that I would get a part.

"You're the best singer in our year," said Jen, who had also auditioned.

"And even if it's just a group part, this is only your first show, Jade," said Laura.

"Everyone knows you can sing," added Britany.

I thought about nothing else over the holiday, which my family did not celebrate, not even with a Christmas tree, and by the time school resumed in January, I was convinced that I would be disappointed when Mr. Gentile posted the cast list on the board in the school hallway.

Two days went by with no announcement, and on the third day, Jen came running over to me in the cafeteria, grinning.

"The list is up," she squealed.

"Oh my god," I said. "Have you seen it? Are we on it?"

"I was waiting for you," said Jen.

We ran straight to the board together, holding hands as we gazed at the sheet of paper that Mr. Gentile had pinned to the cork bulletin board. The first name on the board was Jen, who had been cast as Maria. She screamed, jumping up and down on the spot. A few cast names down the list, I spotted Jade Xiu. I had been cast as Anita. Jen screamed even louder and hugged me tightly.

"I knew it," she said into my hair. "I knew you would get a part."

I was so shocked that I could barely speak. I was Anita. I had a singing part in *West Side Story*. People other than my friends and Mr. Gentile were going to hear me sing. I wasn't even disappointed that I did not get the role of Maria; I was as happy for Jen as I was for myself. I felt as though I could breathe properly for the first time in my life, filling my lungs with sweet life-giving oxygen.

I could sing.

Mr. Gentile believed in me.

Jade Xiu had her first role in a musical, and she was not going to let herself down.

We rehearsed every day after school and even during the weekends, Mr. Gentile giving up his personal time to help the show become the best that it could be. In art class, we designed and photocopied tickets to sell to families and friends. The drama teacher, Miss Reynolds, measured us for costumes and trawled thrift shops for stage props. It seemed the whole school was excited for this production.

As the date grew closer, I spent more and more time in rehearsals, learning my lines, and practicing the songs until I sang them in my sleep. The musical filled my every waking moment. It was the first thing I thought of when I woke, and the last thing I thought of before I fell asleep. I was tired. I woke up even earlier in the mornings to begin my chores at home before school, attending morning rehearsals before homeroom, and then straight back into rehearsals when the final bell of the day rang. Then at home, there were more chores to finish and dinner to prepare before Ma came home.

I had never been happier.

And then one evening the week before the show, my mother told me I needed to be home on time the following Thursday.

I stopped eating and stared at her. Thursday was the night of our production. I wondered if she had found out somehow. Maybe Joseph had told her, although my brother wasn't involved in the show, and I hadn't spoken to him about it.

"Why?" I asked.

"Chinese New Year. There is going to be a festival. Dragons. Lanterns."

"I can't on Thursday, Ma," I said.

My heart was racing. I had never said no to her before; I had never not attended a family event with my parents, not that we went to many.

She turned her beady eyes on me, and I shrank in my seat. "Chinese New Year," she repeated. "We go as a family."

"I can't, Ma."

I looked at Joseph, but he was just staring at both of us as though he didn't understand this unusual turn of events. For all Joseph got away with, a lot more stuff than I did, he never refused to do anything requested of him.

"Why are you saying this?" My mother's voice rose.

"I…," I swallowed "… I am singing in the school production of *West Side Story*."

Joseph watched me as if he didn't recognize his own sister.

"Tell Ma, Joseph." I was pleading with him with my eyes. "Tell Ma there is a show next Thursday at school. You must have seen the posters. You know everyone in school is excited about it."

Our mother looked at Joseph, waiting for him to answer.

He shrugged. "Sure, there is a show next week. I didn't know Jade was singing in it, though."

"I have to sing, Ma. I'm playing Anita. I am a good singer. Mr. Gentile gave me the part because he thinks I'm a good singer. We've been rehearsing since the start of the semester."

"Chinese New Year," she said, her voice cold. "You will come with us."

I was crying now. "I can't let them down, Ma. There is no one else good enough to play Anita."

"You can't let them down?" she spat. "You can't let them down, but you can let your family down for Chinese celebrations?"

"I'll come next time, Ma. I always come with you, I do, but just this once, I can't. I'm sorry, Ma. I'll never let you down again. But this is *West Side Story*. I have to do it." I was sobbing by the time I finished, my tears pooling on top of my food.

My mother grabbed my bowl and tossed it across the kitchen and into the sink, where it smashed to pieces. "You will never say no to me again, Jade. You will come to Chinese New Year, and you will respect your culture."

She grabbed her purse and walked out of the house, leaving me crying at the kitchen table. Joseph did not seem to know what to do, so he went to the sink and began clearing up the mess.

When he was finished, he rubbed my back and said, "Sorry, Jade. I didn't know you could sing."

I didn't speak to my mother for the rest of the week. I attended rehearsals every day. I sang my heart out. My thoughts spun around and around in circles, trying to work out how to explain to her what this meant to me, but each time I pictured the conversation, I knew there was no point.

The day of the show, I dressed for school in the clothes that Jen had given me; I didn't even care if my mother saw them, or if a neighbor told her that they'd seen me looking like a regular kid. The costume I was to wear for Anita was at school, so I didn't need to take anything extra with me as I was planning on not coming home when school finished but staying there until after the show. I knew my mother would be angry, but I also knew she would not come to the school and cause an embarrassing scene. I was scared about the consequences of my actions but had pushed them to the back of my mind until the following day. I would deal with it after.

I wouldn't have had time to go home anyway. We were so busy when the bell rang for the last class, sorting costumes, makeup, hair, reading through lines, making sure everyone was there, that before I knew it, I was Anita, and parents were filling the seats in the main hall where the show was to take place.

Behind the stage, we could hear the hum of conversations, little kids crying, people sneezing and coughing and laughing.

Jen peeped out from behind the curtains and said, "I just saw my parents and Emily."

She looked amazing as Maria, so grownup with her hair curled around her face and wearing red lipstick.

I felt the same pang of jealousy I'd felt when I first met Josephine, that I wished she were my mom, and Jen were my sister, and stepped away from the musty velvet curtains.

"Sorry," she said. "I didn't mean to make you feel bad. I mean, I know your parents can't come."

I had told Jen that my parents had a family Chinese New Year celebration to attend that they couldn't get out of. I could tell what she was thinking: that her parents would have cancelled the other party to come and watch her sing, but she didn't push it. By now, she knew that my mother and father were not like other parents; she had never met them, and she had long ago given up on asking to come to my house.

"It's okay." I forced a smile to my lips and squeezed her hands. "Can you believe we are going to perform in front of all these people?"

"I think I'm going to be sick," said Jen.

"I think I'm going to faint," I said.

Mr. Gentile came and found us and said that we had to be ready in five minutes.

I felt as though I had been ready all my life. When the curtains were pulled aside, and Jen and I walked onto the stage in front of the hushed audience, I forgot about my mother and Chinese lanterns. I forgot about everything but being a star.

The show went so smoothly that it barely felt as though we had been on stage five minutes when the curtains were closing, and the families in the audience were clapping and cheering.

Jen hugged me close and said, "You were amazing, Jade."

I told her that she was the best one. "I could live on the stage," I told her. "I never want to do anything else."

Mr. Gentile was hugging everyone with tears in his eyes. He hugged Jen and I together, an arm around each of us and said, "My two little stars," and in that moment, I felt as though my life was perfect.

That night, when I arrived home, the house was in complete darkness. I guessed my family were still out at the festival, so I washed the makeup from my face in the bathroom, changed into my pajamas, and climbed into bed. I was still staring at the ceiling, too excited to sleep, when they came home at midnight.

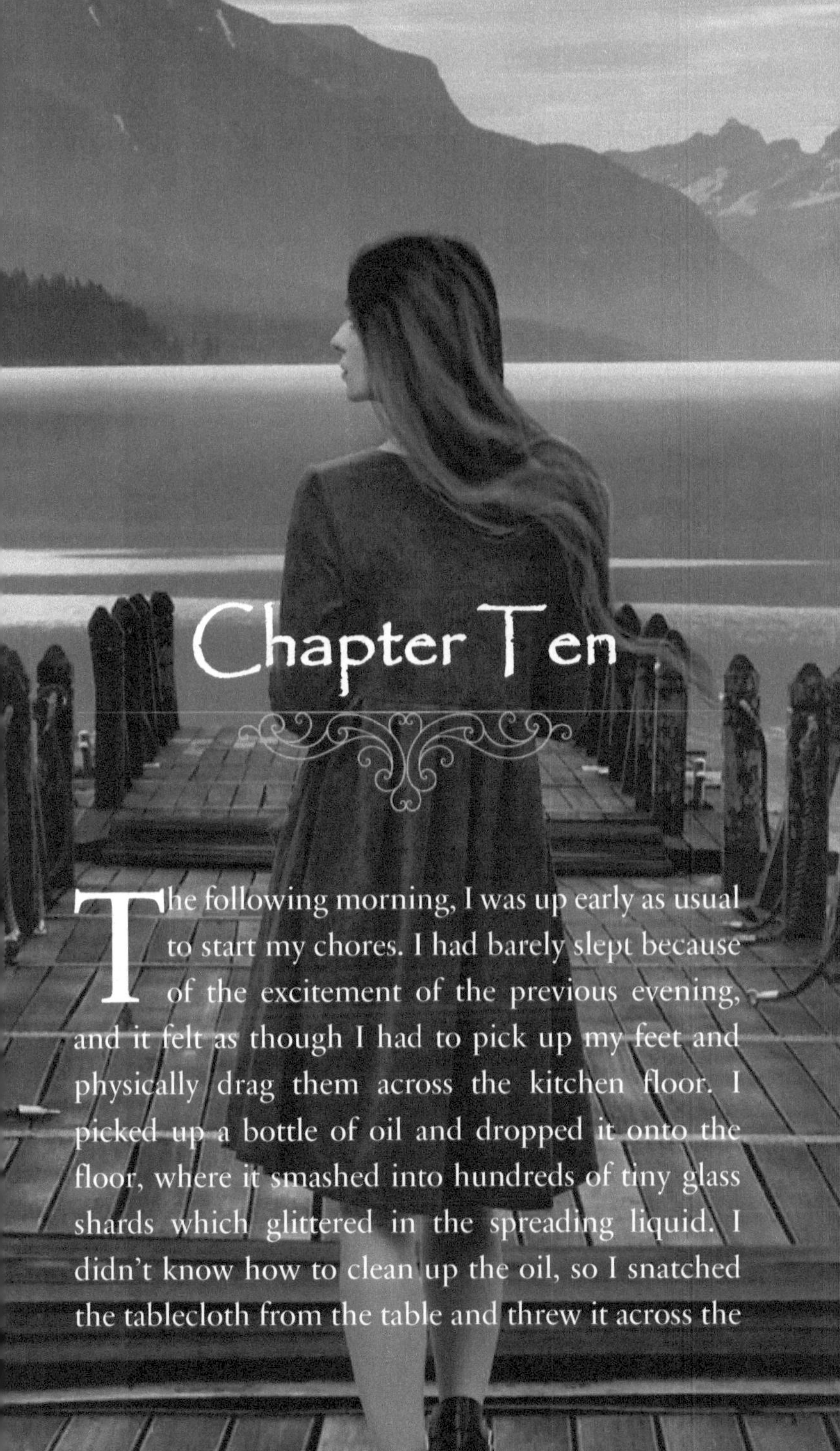

Chapter Ten

The following morning, I was up early as usual to start my chores. I had barely slept because of the excitement of the previous evening, and it felt as though I had to pick up my feet and physically drag them across the kitchen floor. I picked up a bottle of oil and dropped it onto the floor, where it smashed into hundreds of tiny glass shards which glittered in the spreading liquid. I didn't know how to clean up the oil, so I snatched the tablecloth from the table and threw it across the spreading puddle to mop it up, and then had to sit and pick the pieces of glass out of the cloth before putting it in the laundry.

I was still sitting cross-legged on the sticky floor, a pile of glass fragments at my side, and my fingertips bloody and sore, when Joseph walked into the room.

"What are you doing?" he asked, his expression horrified at the mess I had made.

"I'm cleaning up." I was so tired that tears streamed down my face, and I swiped at them, smearing my cheeks with bloody fingerprints.

"Jeez, Jade," said Joseph. "You're bleeding."

I sniffed loudly and picked another piece of glass from the saturated material. "I have to get this out so I can wash it. Ma will go mad when she finds out I smashed the bottle."

Joseph found a dustpan and broom from the cabinet under the sink and scooped up the glass shards, dropping them into the bin. Then he rinsed the cloth under the hot tap to get the worst of the oil out before loading it into the washing machine. I was still sitting on the floor when he asked me how to operate it. I gave him instructions. After, he washed my bleeding fingers in the bathroom and stuck a band-aid on the deepest wound.

"Bet you thought I wasn't domesticated, eh?" he asked.

I nodded. "I've never seen you do anything to help Ma."

He shrugged. "It's because she never asks. Why should I offer my time when I could be out with my friends?"

I thought about it while he patted my sore fingertips dry. "Do they know you have friends?"

"Who?"

"Ma and Pa?"

"Sure."

"No, I mean, have you told them that you have friends at school?"

"What kind of a question is that, Jade?"

"It's the kind of question I need answers to when Ma told me not to bother with friends when I started school."

His eyes flickered from my face to the sink to the bloody towel. Eventually he said, "She wants me to walk you to school today and bring you straight home tonight."

I shook my head and snatched my hand away from his. "She isn't even here. She doesn't even care that I was singing in a show last night, or that singing is what I want to do when I graduate from college.

She won't even be here when I come home from school. So, no!" I stomped my feet in temper.

My fingers were stinging, but it was nothing compared to how angry I was with my mother. She knew nothing about me. She had never been interested in me, and now that I had dared to go against her wishes and miss the Chinese New Year celebration, she wanted to treat me like a baby. I bet she didn't even remember how old I was because we never celebrated birthdays.

"Hey," said Joseph. "I'm on your side. I never said I *was* going to walk you home, did I? I don't want to be seen with you, either." He grinned at me and then pulled my hair.

It eased my mood a little knowing that my brother was still my friend.

We never spoke about the show in our house. Joseph kept his word and didn't chaperone me to and from school, but whenever Ma asked, he told her that I came home with him and sat in my room doing my homework. It was a while before she spoke to me, and when she did, it was only the usual questions about school grades and homework.

Something had shifted between us. I sensed her watching me whenever I was doing the dishes or other chores, as though she was wary about what I would attempt to do next. I spoke to her with the same respect that I always had, only now, I felt as though I had grown muscles, as though she had realized that if I wanted something badly enough, I would do it, with or without her approval. It was a strange feeling, but also a powerful one. I wasn't sure if this was how it felt to be a teenager growing up in America, or if it was just me testing the water for how far I could push her.

The weeks passed by with no need for me to push her further, until one day in the cafeteria, Britany and Laura mentioned summer camp. They were going together. Britany's dad was going to drive them there, and they were talking about all the different activities and sports they would learn while they were there.

"The river runs along the bottom of the camp," said Laura. "There'll be kayaking, white-water rafting, and swimming parties."

"And barbecues and singing in the evenings," added Britany. "My sister goes every summer, and she says the teachers pretty much let you do whatever you want as long as no one is getting drunk."

I sucked in my breath, and Britany stared at me.

"They let you drink alcohol at summer camp?" I asked.

"No," said Britany, "but some of the older kids sneak booze in — my sister said she's going to take a bottle of my dad's gin because he won't miss it — they just keep it hidden and sneak down to the river at night to drink it when the younger kids are in bed."

"Please say you'll both come," said Laura. "It'll be the best summer ever."

"I'll ask my mom tonight," said Jen. They all looked at me. "What do you think your mom will say, Jade? Will she let you go?"

"What do you think?" I asked.

They all shook their heads.

"We need to come up with a plan that she can't refuse," said Jen.

"I don't think she would agree even if Joseph said he was coming with me."

My friends looked at one another, and then they looked at me. "That's not a bad idea," said Jen. "Why don't you ask Joseph to come, too?"

"With us?"

I couldn't believe they would suggest that my big brother, the moody jock who walked around with his fists clenched and his eyebrows lowered, should come with us to summer camp. It would be no fun with him breathing down my neck every minute of every day so that he could report back to my parents.

"No." I shook my head. "No."

"No, not with us, exactly," said Jen. "Although your brother is kind of cute, but he could come to summer camp. Think about it." She widened her eyes at me like she couldn't believe I hadn't yet gotten the point. "If they agree to let Joseph go, how can they say no to you?"

I smiled at my friend. It was a good point. I still wasn't convinced Joseph would go along with it, or even if he did, that my parents would follow the same logic as my friends, but I didn't have a better suggestion.

"Is that a yes?" asked Britany.

"We can try." I shrugged.

I had nothing to lose other than a summer with my friends if the plan didn't work.

We hung around the field waiting for Joseph to finish football practice. He was so engrossed, he didn't notice us until they all started walking back toward the locker room, and then he stopped when he realized I was one of the four girls staring at him.

"Jade?" he asked. "What are you doing here? What's wrong?"

"Nothing's wrong," I said. "We just want to talk to you about something."

"Hi, Joseph." My friends waved at him and giggled.

He barely glanced at them.

I took a deep breath, feeling awkward because he was waiting for me to speak. Some boys on the field behind him began jeering and whistling, and Joseph ignored them.

"Will you ask Ma if you can go to summer camp?"

His eyes narrowed, and now he looked at my friends properly for the first time. I wished I could read his mind because it was impossible to tell what he was thinking as he took in their clothes and their hair and their smiles. He returned his gaze to me.

"Why?" he asked.

"Because I want to go, Joseph. Everyone else is going, and I don't want to be stuck here all summer on my own with no one to talk to and chores to do every day. Ma will tell me to study, and I don't want to spend my summer studying while everyone else is swimming and having fun and making new friends.”

“So, why do you want me to go?”

“Because if Ma agrees to let you go, she can’t say no to me.”

I was panting, my heart beating crazily. I hadn’t realized how important this was to me until I started telling Joseph, and now I knew that I couldn’t let them go without me. I felt like if they did, our friendships would be over by the time they came back because they would have formed a different alliance that didn’t include me.

“Jade,” Joseph went to walk away, “we’ll talk about this later.”

“No!” I grabbed his arm, and he stopped and stared at my hand.

“Please, Joseph,” said Jen. “Will you at least think about it? I’m sure you’ll have fun too if you came.”

Joseph’s gaze flickered between Jen and me. “I *am* going,” he said.

It was several moments before I realized what he had said. “Wait, what?” I mumbled. “What do you mean? You will ask Ma if you can go?”

“No. I mean, I *have* already asked Ma, and I *am* going to summer camp.”

"Yay!" squealed Britany. "That means you can come, Jade."

But I felt no excitement. My heart lurched, making me feel nauseous. If Joseph was already going, it meant that my parents had not even considered sending me there also; it meant that they had happily paid for Joseph and assumed that Yù would be at home doing everything around the house so that they didn't have to.

Joseph must have sensed my thought process and the logical conclusion I had reached. "I'll speak to you later, Jade," he repeated and walked back into the school building.

Jen watched him walk away. "You don't think they'll let you go?" she asked.

I shook my head. I needed a plan B.

My father was home early that evening. We sat at the table to eat dinner together, and I kept my eyes on my food as usual while we ate in silence. I kept thinking about what to say, about how to ask them if I could go to summer camp. I had no idea how Joseph had managed to persuade them, unless they believed that it was an extension of school studies. I ran through different ways of broaching the subject in my head until the words were all jumbled up like the pieces of a jigsaw puzzle still in the box.

My father finished his food first and pushed his bowl away from him. He went to leave the table, so I blurted it out. "Can I go to summer camp?"

He stopped, his hands on the edge of the table, ready to slide his chair backwards. He asked my mother, "Is summer camp for girls?"

She stared at me with narrowed eyes, as if accusing me of stirring trouble for her again like I was the most troublesome daughter to ever have existed in the history of time, and she didn't understand why she had been unlucky enough to deserve me.

"No," she said. "For boys."

"That isn't true, Ma. The other girls in my class are going." I looked at Joseph, begging him with my eyes to back me up.

He cleared his throat. "It's for boys and girls," he said.

"Where do they stay?" asked my father. He was speaking to my mother, not to us.

"In cabins," said Joseph. "There are separate cabins for boys and girls. It's all pretty standard. What do you think...?" he hesitated, choosing his words carefully. "... There are plenty of adults working at the camp."

They were silent. When I was a little girl, I sometimes wondered if parents communicated by telepathy because they seemed to know what the other was thinking without saying anything out loud, but by this point, I had realized that my father was waiting for my mother to make the decisions.

"No," she said.

It was a short and snappy word that echoed in my ears after she said it.

"Why not, Ma?" I asked. "Pa? Why not?" I had never played my parents off against each other before, but I was desperate. Why was I not allowed to ask my father? Jen would not have been scared to ask her dad if she wanted to go somewhere.

"I need you here," my mother said.

"You don't need me here. I never see you because you're always working. You don't know what classes I have. You don't see what homework I do. You didn't even come to watch me perform in the musical."

My father blinked at me several times as though he had no idea what I was talking about. I should have taken their silence as a warning, but I was on a roll now, filled with the injustice of the way they treated me differently compared to my brother.

"You came to America to escape the Chinese regime and to be free, and yet you still act like you live in Beijing. I am not you, Ma! I am not growing up in China where I have to be quiet and study until I become a pharmacist because it is what *you* want. You came here to give your children the opportunities you never had, but what opportunities are you giving me?" My chest was heaving.

"You are getting a decent education," my mother said slowly. "You should be grateful—"

I didn't let her finish. "Okay, so why is Joseph going to summer camp?"

Her eyes did not waver from mine. Finally, she said in a quiet voice, "Enough, Yù."

But I wasn't finished. "He is getting a decent education. Why is that not enough for him?"

"Enough!" My mother stood and pointed at the doorway. "Go to your room!"

Tears streaked my face. I shoved my chair backwards, toppling it onto the floor, and ran to my room where I lied on my bed with my face buried in my pillow.

I considered running away. I thought about waiting until they were all asleep, stuffing the clothes Jen gave to me into my backpack, and tiptoeing out the door and into the night. I imagined walking out of town with the moon and stars for company. I had no idea where I would go or whether I would be eaten by wild animals while I slept, but at that moment, it was preferable to being a Chinese American girl who was destined for a lifetime of studying and working and being alone.

I thought about Joseph. I rarely passed him in the school hallways, but whenever I did see him, he was usually alone. I had never considered the possibility that life might be difficult for him as well because his life at home was so easy, but now I wondered if he had friends, or at least one good friend, the way I had Jen. I wished our parents would listen to us. Then they might understand that in order for us to have the freedom they claimed they wanted us to have, we needed to learn how to be American.

I heard the clatter of my mother in the kitchen, doing the dishes and tidying up. Joseph must have gone to his room because I heard the murmur of my parents' voices, low enough that I couldn't pick out the individual words.

I must have dozed, my brain exhausted with thoughts of running away and living in the woods somewhere out of town. I stirred when my bedroom door opened, whispering against the carpet, light from the hallway spilling onto my face. I rolled over, my face sticky with tears and dribble, and saw my mother walk into the room and sit on the end of the bed.

I sat up and waited for her to speak.

"Yù, I have spoken to your father. He has decided that you can go to summer camp with Joseph."

I blinked, my eyelashes sticking together with sleep. I wasn't sure if I was dreaming, but I allowed a smile to spread across my face.

"We want you to have freedom; we are just scared that you will stop caring about your education and stop having respect for us and your heritage."

"That will never happen, Ma," I said. "I promise."

"You should never make promises you not know you can keep, Jade," she said, using my American name.

I wanted to throw my arms around her neck and hug her, but she was already on her feet and walking back toward the door.

"Ma," I said, "thank you."

She smiled and closed the door behind her.

Struggle Between Two Lives

Chapter Eleven

rriving at summer camp was like stepping into a picture or onto the set of a movie. The sun was shining through the trees and making the river sparkle, and everything smelled so fresh and alive. I spotted Jen straight off, standing with a group of other girls, her rucksack at her feet. She was waiting for her name to be ticked off at registration by a guy in shorts and a T-shirt with the slogan Rowantree Campers and a silhouette of a tree on the front. I smiled at Jen, and she smiled back, but she knew we wouldn't be able to speak until my parents had left.

Joseph lifted our bags from the trunk of Pa's car. Pa shook his hand and then turned to me and gave me a brief hug. It was the only contact I could ever remember having with my father, and it made tears well in my eyes. My mother hugged Joseph first. She looked at me and held my shoulders.

"Do not forget your studies, Yù," she said.

I wasn't sure if she entirely understood what summer camp was about, but I told her that I wouldn't anyway. Then she squeezed me against her chest and kissed the top of my head.

And then they were gone.

We watched the car drive away. "I can see Jen over there," I said to Joseph, pointing at the line where Jen was still somewhere near the end.

Joseph nodded but didn't move.

"Are your friends meeting you here?" I asked.

Joseph grinned. "Are you worried about me?"

I smiled back. "No, you're supposed to worry about me. You're the eldest."

"I do," he said. "I'll see you around, then."

He hoisted his bag onto his shoulder and headed off toward a group of boys who looked around the same age as him. I guessed it wouldn't do him any favors being seen with his kid sister.

I ran over to Jen and hugged her, both of us jumping up and down on the spot. It was like arriving at the park for a six-week-long picnic, believing that the sun would shine every day, and the food would be diner-worthy with no parents telling us to eat our vegetables.

When we reached the front of the line, the guy, whose name was Jacob, told us to call him Jake and that we were staying in the Cedar cabin together. I was so happy, I felt like I might burst. I had been worried about having to share a room with a bunch of girls I'd never met before, so this was like ordering a chocolate chip muffin with extra chocolate. It was perfect.

When we were eventually shown to the cabin, which was nestled amongst the trees close to the hut where we would be eating our meals, we were shocked to see that Laura and Britany were already there.

They came running over and almost knocked us backwards with their exuberance. "I can't believe they put us all together," said Laura. "We're going to party every night."

Once we had unpacked, we all made our way to a clearing at the center of the camp, which was where Jake told us we would meet up every morning and be allocated the day's schedule of activities. There were lots of kids already there, sitting on the grass or on logs arranged in a circle around the outside of the clearing like an outdoor auditorium.

I was buzzing inside and could barely concentrate on what my friends were saying. I had no idea how I would ever pay attention to the camp leaders, or how I would find my way back to the cabin alone. Jen, Laura, and Britany, although they had never been here before, seemed to naturally understand what to expect and how to behave. They were relaxed. They found a spot on the grass and sat cross-legged while waiting for everyone else to join us when they had finished unpacking.

I saw Joseph across the clearing with another boy I vaguely recognized from school. Seeing Joseph there with his baseball cap turned backwards and his football shirt on, I was struck by the realization that my brother had done everything I had done to fit in, and yet he still looked different, set apart from the others, and I couldn't work out whether he thought the same about me.

Did I still look different? Since starting high school, building my friendship group, and singing in the musical, I had assumed that I was just like any other girl in school. But now I glanced around, and I knew that I wasn't. Joseph and I were the only Asian American kids here.

It was like a shadow passing over me. The girls' voices seemed to slide away, and I hugged my knees to my chest to stop myself from shivering. Now that I had thought of it, I couldn't unthink it. Glancing around, I felt as though everyone was staring at me, wondering what I was doing here when I should be at home stir-frying noodles. I rested my chin on my knees and closed my eyes to stop the tears from flowing.

"Jade? Are you okay?" I felt Jen's arm wrap around my shoulders.

"I'm fine," I said with a tiny voice.

"Are you sure? You don't look it."

"Is it because there are lots of kids here?" asked Laura. "It's a bit loud and overwhelming. My mom always says to imagine everyone naked, and then you don't feel nearly as bad about yourself."

"Um, that's just gross," said Britany.

Jen laughed.

I smiled at Laura; she often knew the right thing to say, and I sometimes wondered if she felt a little bit left out of things with Britany being so loud and lively.

"Thank you," I said.

I was here now. I needed to do what my mother always said — hold my head high and get on with it.

It wasn't long before Jake was standing in the middle of the circle with his clipboard. He was with three other camp leaders: Brian, Sonia, and Julia, who were also all holding clipboards.

"Welcome to Rowantree," said Jake. He was good looking, cute with dark hair that flopped over his eyes so that he had to keep jerking his head back to move it. He introduced himself and the other leaders. "We are going to be splitting you up into teams," he said. "You will stay in your allocated teams throughout the summer and whenever you are taking part in activities. You might notice a little bit of friendly rivalry along the way. I just want to say that you can put in as much or as little effort as you want, as long as my team wins."

All the kids laughed. The other leaders shook their heads and gave him a thumbs-down. I realized I felt better already. I just hoped that I was on the same team as my friends.

The teams were called: Harper, Steinbeck, Twain, and Plath.

"I know, I know," said Jake. "We're raising the standards this year, kids. You look like you're all up for a challenge. Am I right?"

The kids cheered.

"Am I right?" Jake yelled, louder this time.

The kids all cheered and clapped, and some even whistled with their fingers in their mouth. The excitement was contagious, and my fears were already subsiding. Jake said he was going to call out our names, and we were to join our respective leaders who would give us a schedule of activities and competitions that would take place throughout the summer.

"We'll reconvene here tonight, after supper," he said. "There are camp rules that we need you to follow at all times, but we don't want to hit you with the boring stuff straight away."

He called out the names. Britany and Laura were both in Twain. I could tell that they were happy to be together. I knew we were in the same cabin, but it would be nice if we were all on the same team during the day, too. Joseph and I were both in Plath.

There was only Jen to go. I waited behind Julia, my fingers crossed behind my back, and murmured under my breath, "Please let it be Plath. Please let it be Plath."

When Jen's name was called out, followed by the word *Twain*, my stomach twisted. She ran to join Britany and Laura, and it wasn't until they had hugged each other that she turned to me and mouthed, 'Sorry.' It wasn't her fault. I knew that, but I couldn't help feeling like being in competition against my friends all summer was going to change things.

"Alright, Jade?" It was Joseph.

I nodded.

He glanced at the group of kids now known as Twain. "Hey, you've got me."

He made his eyebrows dance comically. I had no idea how he did that, but it made me smile.

"And me," said a voice behind me.

I turned around to see a boy who was a little taller than me, although I recognized him from school as being the year above me. I didn't know his name, though.

"Aaron," he said. "My friends are in Harper with Jake. Looks like we need to knock them off the top spot this year."

Joseph moved to stand protectively beside me.

"Sounds good to me," I said.

We spent the first afternoon playing silly games and getting to know each other. Dinner was louder and busier than the cafeteria in school, but because there was no pressure of classes and teachers breathing down our necks, the hum of voices and scraping of chairs only added to my excitement.

I was at summer camp! Me — Jade Xiu — I had somehow made it to summer camp with my friends, which meant six weeks of not having to avoid my parents and make excuses about where I was going or where I had been.

That first night in the cabin in the woods, we were awake for hours, whispering and giggling and making plans. For that first blissful evening, it didn't matter that we had been divided into different groups — we were friends, and it wasn't like we attended the same classes in school.

We woke up early the next morning to the sun streaming through the cabin windows. We had toast and muffins and fruit and hot chocolate for breakfast, and I decided right then that it was going to be my favorite meal of the day.

The first activity of the summer, and one in which the groups would be competing against each other, was kayaking. I was paired up with Aaron, who grinned at me as if he had planned it that way all along. Jen, Laura, and Britany were also paired up with boys, which made me feel better because I knew Joseph couldn't say anything about me being with a boy if everyone else was also in a boy-girl coupling.

I'd never noticed before, but Aaron was strong for a boy who was smaller than most other boys his age. He'd obviously done kayaking before. We spent some time practicing, getting in and out of the kayaks and learning what to do if we capsized, and then each pair took turns racing the other teams along the river to a flag in the distance and back again. Twain was in the lead by one point when it was my turn with Aaron. We were up against Jen and her partner from Twain.

I could tell straight off that Jen wasn't feeling that confident; she stumbled climbing into the kayak and almost fell into the water, which made me gasp. She grimaced at me, and I gave her an encouraging smile. When the teams were lined up and waiting for the whistle, I could hear Jen's partner telling her what to do. Her face was pale. I felt sorry for her and couldn't wait for the evening when we could sit on our beds and laugh about the day's activities.

The whistle sounded, and we were moving away and already in the lead, mainly because of Aaron. We reached the flag ahead of the other teams. As we were turning, I saw that Jen and her partner were drifting toward the reeds lining the river. The boy was yelling at her, and I wasn't certain because my bangs were in my eyes, but it looked like she was crying.

I glanced behind me at Aaron.

"Keep your eyes straight ahead," he said. "We're going to win, Jade."

But I couldn't stop glancing over my shoulder, and I could see that Jen was crying. She wasn't even paddling, and her partner was frantically trying to get them back on track.

"Jen!" I yelled. "Use your paddle."

She peered around at me and blinked as if she didn't even know how she had come to be there.

"We have to go help them," I said to Aaron over my shoulder.

"No!" he said. "She has a partner. He can turn them around. We'll lose if we stop."

It was true. I could see Julia and the rest of the Plath team jumping up and down on the riverbank, cheering and shouting, "Go Jade! Go Aaron!" We would be the first pair to win a race for Plath today if we made it back first, and I knew that we would lose if we stopped to help Jen. I was torn. I could see that my friend was upset, but winning a race was the first step toward me fitting in at summer camp and being a part of a team. This was a competition. Someone had to lose. And it wasn't like I was responsible for Jen.

I mouthed the word 'Sorry' to her and paddled as hard as I could toward the finish line.

The other kids on our team hugged us when we climbed out of the kayak. Julia hugged us too, a wide grin on her flushed face, and said, "I knew I had the winning team this year." Everyone patted our backs, and even Jake came over and shook our hands.

The only person who didn't congratulate us was Jen. When they eventually paddled back to shore, she climbed out of the kayak and stood with Britany and Laura, who hugged her and stroked her hair. They turned and walked back toward the shower cabins without a glance in my direction.

Aaron squeezed my hands and said, "You were great, Jade. Good job!"

When I nodded and blinked back the tears that were collecting on my eyelashes, he followed my gaze toward my friends, whose backs were visible and wrapped in towels as they disappeared into the showers.

"It does get a bit competitive," he said, "but they'll come around. We're all in this together."

I sat with Aaron at lunch and didn't even see the girls. I didn't know if they just weren't hungry, or if they grabbed some food and ate outside, but I was grateful that Aaron wanted to spend some time with me. I had spent enough lunches eating alone in elementary school to know that I didn't want to do it again, especially not here when we were supposed to be having fun.

We spent the afternoon painting, large sheets of paper spread out on easels overlooking the river, before helping the camp assistants tidy the paints and brushes and other equipment away. I wanted to keep busy to take my mind off Jen. I hoped she wasn't angry with me, but there was no denying that they have been avoiding me since the race — why else would they not have asked me to join them?

I finally caught up with them at dinner. They were already eating when I carried my tray across to the end of the long refectory table where they were seated.

"Are you okay?" I asked Jen. She glanced at me and gave me a brief nod. "I'm sorry I couldn't help earlier. I wanted to. But Aaron said your partner could manage."

She peered at me without speaking, and my stomach twisted. She couldn't be angry with me, not on our first day, and I hadn't done anything wrong.

"It's alright," she said eventually. "Brad was being a moron and yelling at me. I thought you were going to stop."

"I was," I said. "Honest."

"It was only a race, Jade," said Britany, biting a mouthful of burger. "It would have been nice to put your friend first."

I chewed my bottom lip and waited for her to smooth over her cross words with a smile, but she didn't. I felt like asking Britany if she would have stopped if I was stuck in the reeds, but I felt embarrassed enough, and I didn't want this to turn into a full-blown argument, so I nodded, and said, "Sorry," and forced my dinner down my throat, although my appetite had flown away.

That night, after the camp leaders came around and told us it was time for lights out, there were no whispering or giggles or climbing into bed together and huddling beneath the blankets. I lied awake for hours after they were asleep, staring at the stars through the window and trying to convince myself that nothing had changed.

Chapter Twelve

The girls didn't ignore me over the following weeks, but something had shifted between us, and I couldn't explain how it was different or why it had happened. It was almost as though they had been happy being my friend while I was the poor little Asian girl whom everyone ignored and didn't have a life, but the moment I became the Jade who was good at something and part of a team, they treated me the way they treated other girls.

By frowning down upon me because my clothes were secondhand. By rolling their eyes each time I won another competition. By putting up with me at mealtimes and then scampering away when it was time to sit around the campfire so that I couldn't find them.

I told myself repeatedly that I was being paranoid. I had seen the way the popular girls in school treated the other girls, including us, and I didn't want to believe that my friends could behave the same way. But it seemed that my acceptance by everyone else had erected a barrier between us that I didn't know how to overcome.

When I found wild blackberries growing in the woods, I gathered some because I knew Jen liked them, washed them carefully in the water fountain, and set them in a neat pile on the small cabinet beside Jen's bed so that she would find them when it was nighttime. She sat on the edge of her bed and glanced around when she saw them. She caught my eye. I smiled at her, and she gave me a silent 'Thank you' in return.

But when she popped one into her mouth, I heard Britany say, "Ugh! What's that crawling down the side of your cabinet," and she chucked the pile of berries out the window.

Another time, I was asked if I would like to help out in the kitchen and show the cooks how to make Asian food. The camp leaders were excited, and even got the kids to design a special menu in the afternoon's art class, which they hung on the wall in the cafeteria.

For the first time, I felt kind of proud of my culture and was grateful that I had always helped my mother cook. We made fried rice, noodles, spicy chicken, and dumplings. It smelled as good as Ma's cooking, and I couldn't wait for the other kids to try it.

Some kids dove straight in. Aaron looked over at me and gave me a thumbs up — he knew that I had been helping prepare the meal and told me he was excited to try Chinese food for the first time. Other kids wrinkled their noses and pushed the noodles around their plates as if they had been given a plate of worms.

When I took my seat with my friends, I was happy to see that Jen was eating her food. As soon as I sat down and breathed in the spicy aroma, Britany said, "I don't know how you eat this stuff all the time. Give me a hot dog any day."

Jen chewed her food slowly. Laura glanced away and picked at a bit of chicken. Neither of them said anything when Britany sat back with her arms crossed and refused to eat.

I saw Joseph around the camp often. He mostly seemed to be by himself, head down, or tagging along behind a group of other boys who nudged and jostled each other, without including him in their banter. I couldn't worry about him, though. I had enough to think about with my friends acting so weird. I had worked out that whatever had happened, it was mostly down to Britany.

Whenever I saw Jen alone, she was the same girl I had been friends with since elementary school, but the moment she saw Britany and Laura, her attitude changed, and she developed a way of peering at me from the corner of her eye, or with her chin raised in the air as though I were a silly little kid to be avoided.

I was grateful for Aaron.

I didn't know why he had decided to befriend me on the first day, but after a few weeks, I realized I only felt comfortable around him. He made me laugh. He told me stories about his family — he had four older brothers who all picked on him, and his grandparents also lived with them, which caused problems because they were both deaf, and the dog kept stealing their glasses and burying them in the garden. Aaron made me feel normal. He laughed at me when I was clumsy and spilled ketchup on my T-shirt, and praised me when I did something well or learned something new.

There was an end-of-summer show in which every kid would take part, and Aaron and I were awarded the lead roles, which meant that we got to spend even more time together rehearsing our lines and learning the songs.

The week before the show, Joseph pulled me aside one evening after dinner.

"What's going on with you and Aaron?" he asked.

"What do you mean?" I glared at him until he removed his hand from my arm.

"Everyone is talking about you. You have spent more time with him than with your friends."

I shook my head. "I don't understand. Aaron *is* my friend. Why should anyone talk about that? I've seen you with Katy Donaldson, and no one is talking about that."

"That's different," he said.

"Why? Why is that different?"

"I'm older than you, and I'm a boy."

I could not believe what my brother was saying. My blood was raging through my veins, but I didn't want him saying anything to our parents when we went home; I would never be allowed to come again if they knew. I would never be allowed anywhere. It was the first time I had even considered the fact that Aaron was a boy, and that people might misunderstand our friendship, and it felt like someone had washed the day away with a bucket of muddy water.

"Katy is a girl," I said, keeping my voice low. "I don't hear anyone talking about her. Not that it would make you stay away from her. You're a boy — you can obviously do what you want." I turned to walk away.

"Jade!" said Joseph. "Come back here."

I whirled around. "You're not Pa," I snapped. "And if I hear anyone speaking about me, I'll tell them Aaron is my friend."

After, I listened to conversations whenever I passed a group of kids, but I didn't hear anything or see anyone whispering about me behind their hands. I'd had enough practice avoiding people's stares and pointing fingers to know when to keep my head down, and I believed Joseph was making it up.

The show was a success. Again, I had the sense that I was born to be on stage, and that if I could spend the rest of my life performing, I would be the happiest person alive.

With two days left before the end of summer camp, the leaders announced that we would be having a party on the final night, with a barbecue by the river, music, and swimming. Although I couldn't swim, Jen had given me a bathing suit to bring to summer camp, knowing that there would be the opportunity to swim in the river. Jen was taller and slimmer than I was, and the swimsuit felt snug when I put it on, pulling my body in and pushing it out in all the right places.

I felt more self-conscious in the swimsuit than I did on a stage singing in front of an audience. When I stepped outside of the changing rooms, Jen's eyes widened.

"Wow!" she said, "It suits you."

The others didn't say anything, but I saw a half-smile on Britany's face as she whispered behind her fingers to Laura.

Aaron was already by the river with his friends. When he saw me, he came running over and gave me a hug, swinging me around in a circle and off my feet.

"We've set up a rope swing," he said. "You girls joining us?"

I glanced around at Jen, who glanced at Britany, waiting for her approval. Britany shrugged, and we followed Aaron's group. They had formed a circle around a pile of soda cans and towels. As we approached them, a tall boy named David ran toward the river's edge while holding a thick rope in his hands, leapt over the water, and dropped the rope once he was swinging above the middle of the river. The splash soaked us all.

Britany took a deep breath and straightened her now damp hair.

Aaron laughed. "Wanna try it next?" he asked me.

I shook my head. "I can't swim."

"I'll go next," said Britany.

She caught the rope easily as it sprang back and copied what David had done, running and jumping into the river, holding tightly onto the rope. Her splash was smaller but still reached us all. Aaron cheered. Laura went next.

Jen was eying where they were splashing in the water with David and some other boys.

"It's okay, you can go next," I said.

She hesitated, watching my face, and it felt like the first time we had been alone together since we arrived.

"Are you sure, Jade?" she asked.

I nodded. "I'll be fine."

I wanted to add that I'd hardly spent any time with them anyway, but I didn't want my comment to spoil the party.

Aaron stood beside me and watched as Jen ran toward the river, releasing the rope too soon, and almost landing on David's head.

"I've got a great idea," he said. "Come with me." He took my hand and started heading downstream.

"Where are we going?" I asked.

"I'm going to teach you how to swim," he said.

"No," I shook my head. "I'm not sure I can."

"Why not?" he stopped, still holding my hand, and waited for me to explain.

Tears welled in my eyes, and he reached up and brushed them away with his fingertips.

"I don't know," I said. "I think I would rather just watch."

He took a deep breath, held my arms in both his hands, and said, "Jade Xiu, I have watched those girls treat you like crap since we got here, and I am not going to sit back and watch them do it again today. Now, you can go back and watch them have fun without you, or you can let me show you how to swim. I'm no expert, but if I can teach you to float and move forward, then I'll consider that a success, wouldn't you?"

I laughed, nodded, and cried all at the same time, and Aaron pretended not to notice.

We waded into the water until it reached our waists.

"Okay," he said. "First things first, you need to get wet. So, let's just dip our heads beneath the surface." He dropped suddenly to demonstrate and resurfaced, shaking the water from his hair. "Your turn."

I copied Aaron, but as I bent my knees, I lost my footing and stumbled forward, arms thrashing the water. When Aaron grabbed my arms and pulled me up, I was coughing and spluttering, my hair plastered to my face.

"Alright?" he asked. "That was one way of doing it."

He wasn't laughing at me, though. He was a patient instructor, and it wasn't long before I was confident enough to lift my feet off the riverbed, with him supporting my stomach, and swim a few strokes.

"That's it. Now this time, I'll take my arms away, so don't panic, okay?"

I nodded. It was such an unusual feeling, floating on the water's surface. I felt as though it had opened up a whole new world to me, almost like someone had said, "Okay, there's the sky, now go fly."

We went back to the party. Aaron swung first into the river using the makeshift rope-swing, and then I followed him, screaming as I landed with a splash.

"Jade!" Jen shrieked. "I didn't know you could swim."

"Aaron taught me!"

I was laughing as one of Aaron's friends splashed me from behind. I was having so much fun, I didn't notice Britany and Laura going back to sit with the others on the riverbank.

It wasn't until later, when we were sitting around the firepit eating burnt sausages and chicken wings, and the team leaders were playing guitar and singing folk songs, that I noticed Britany and Laura watching me and whispering behind their hands to some other girls who were sitting close to them.

Jen spotted them at the same time. "What the hell?!" she said. "Are they talking about us?"

"No, they're talking about me."

Joseph appeared behind us and tapped me on the shoulder. He wasn't smiling.

"Can I have a word with you?" he said.

I shook my head. "Not now, Joseph. Everyone's looking."

He turned to Aaron, who was sitting on the other side of me. "Why don't you stay away from my sister?"

Aaron's gaze flickered between us. He rose to his feet and said, "Hey, bro, what's going on? She's my friend, I—"

But Joseph wasn't listening. He shoved Aaron backwards, and he nearly stumbled onto someone's lap.

Jen and I both jumped up. I pushed Joseph away from Aaron, my chest heaving with anger. "What are you doing?" I asked through clenched teeth. "Go back to your friends, and leave me alone."

Joseph's face paled despite the healthy glow he had caught over the summer. "Not while you're acting like a slut."

It felt as though he had punched me in the stomach. I was gasping for air and clutching at Jen's hands.

Jen stood tall and said, "You obviously don't know your sister at all. If you choose to believe silly childish rumors spread by jealous girls over your sister, then I feel sorry for you."

Joseph didn't seem to know what to say. He dropped his clenched fists and walked away. Aaron joined me and Jen back on the grass, and the three of us sat quietly, staring at Britany and Laura until they got up and walked away.

"It was them, wasn't it?" I asked Jen.

She nodded. "I'm sorry, Jade. I knew they were jealous because you seemed to be having so much fun, but I didn't realize they would go this far."

"It's okay," I said. I was happy that we were friends again.

It seemed to mark a new beginning of my friendship with Jen, and one that now included Aaron. I had never dared to befriend a boy before, because despite my obsession with TV shows like *Saved by the Bell*, I knew my parents would never understand and react the same way that Joseph had. It was beyond their comprehension for girls and boys to be friends.

Because I was a girl, my life plan was study-work-marriage. So, although Joseph also had friends who were girls, he never brought them home or spoke about them. In fact, neither of us ever introduced anyone to our parents. It was as though we were closed books whose pages only ever turned while we were outside of the family home.

Chapter Thirteen

When Joseph left for college, I felt even more lonely. It was as though my parents switched off completely without my brother and forgot they still had a teenage daughter at home. The conversation became non-existent. I was certain that if anyone had asked my parents about me, they'd have said, "Jade… who?"

Jen and Aaron became my substitute family as we progressed through high school. My mother worked fewer hours, so I took a job at a salon during the weekends sweeping up hair. With the few dollars I earned, I bought clothes. I became a pro at scouring the thrift shops and picking up bargains, adapting them to the style I wanted, which was kind of a hippy rock star look.

I still wore my homemade clothes around the house and walked to Jen's each morning before school to change into my real-Jade clothes. I had become a permanent fixture in Jen's house, and if anything, I felt more at home there than I did in my own home.

I hadn't given up my dream of being a rock star. I sang in all the school productions alongside Aaron and Jen, and my parents never came to watch. Because there were no rock star courses offered at my school, I had continued studying chemistry and biology, mainly as a concession to my parents' wishes, but also because Aaron took the same subjects, and he was still having fun. He wanted to play football, but I guess he'd worked out that he needed a fallback profession in case it didn't work out. Jen was more creative than we were and wanted to go to design school. It meant that she had a lot of different classes, but we always met up for lunch in the cafeteria and after school every day to gossip and laugh and just hang out as best friends.

We were inseparable.

Until Logan came to our school.

We were standing by the lockers one morning when he walked past, flanked by two boys from our year's basketball team, who may as well have been invisible for how much attention I gave them. It was like watching a movie scene in slow mo, the way he walked, a bag slung over one shoulder, wearing a black T-shirt and blue jeans, his hair slicked back, his blue eyes looking as though they had been painted on.

I held my breath until Aaron placed his hands on my shoulders from behind and whispered in my ear, "I think Jen's in love."

The world sped up, and I glanced at Jen, who was still watching Logan, openmouthed. When he disappeared into a classroom, she said, "Oh. My. God. Who is that?"

We didn't find out Logan's name until later that day in English literature class when the teacher introduced him. We never did find out why he had transferred in the final year of high school, but that was because we didn't care enough to ask. He was beautiful. He was clever. And it was love at first sight for Jen.

We were in very few classes together, but it seemed that everywhere we went, Logan went, too. Aaron seemed totally oblivious to the boy's charms; I guess because he was also a boy. But because he hung around us, I expected him to feel the same emotions that we felt.

We walked out of the chemistry lab, and he was there. We headed down to the football field to watch Aaron, and he would be there, sitting across from us in the bleachers, always surrounded by other kids. It was as though he came with a ready-made group of friends.

One day at lunch, I was in the cafeteria with Aaron while waiting for Jen to join us. He was talking about a movie showing at the cinema that weekend starring John Cusack that he wanted to see, when I glanced up and saw Jen making her way over to us. She smiled when she spotted us. Someone sitting at another table called her, and as she turned around with her tray in her hands, she collided with Logan. The tray landed on the floor, spilling pasta salad and orange juice everywhere.

Jen's face crumpled, and she dropped to her knees as Logan dropped to his, their foreheads bashing together.

"Ow!" Jen sat back on her heels, one hand pressed to her forehead.

Logan grinned. "I'm sorry." I heard him say. "I should've been watching where I was going. Stay there!" he added when she tried to pick up her spilled food. "Let me clean it up, and then I'll buy you another lunch."

She looked at me above his head and raised her eyebrows.

Aaron had heard the commotion and was watching over his shoulder. "Smooth move," he said, turning back. "Although clumsy probably isn't her best look."

I nodded. I didn't know why, but I kind of wished it had been me Logan had collided with.

By the time Jen joined us with a fresh pasta salad, she was grinning. "You'll never guess what just happened," she said, taking a seat beside me.

"Hmmm, you ran into Logan and dropped your food all over the floor?" said Aaron with a sly smile.

"Not that," said Jen, although she was still smiling. "Logan asked me out on a date. Can you believe it?" she squealed. Her cheeks were pink, she sounded breathless, and I felt the first pangs of jealousy.

No one had ever asked me out on a date, not that I would have been allowed to go, but anyway, first dates and kisses were all I seemed to read about these days. I was obsessed with historical romance novels, and in particular, the *Angelique* series by Anne Golon, which Jen's mom had introduced me to. They were filled with passion and steamy kisses and pirates, and I found myself blushing whenever I read a few pages.

"What do you think, Jade?" asked Aaron.

"Huh?"

"We could all go to the cinema this weekend, a double date."

I nodded. "Sure."

"I'll tell Logan when I see him after school," said Jen. "Oh my god, I'm so excited."

We met outside the cinema in town Saturday afternoon. I told my mother I was working late, and she didn't question it. Studying, working, these things were permitted for a young Chinese American girl. It never struck me until I was older how little control they had over my free time for such controlling parents; at the time, I baulked at the need to tell them where I was every minute of every day. I was certain that, given the opportunity, they'd have paid a private detective to follow me around.

Aaron put his arms around me and gave me a hug when he arrived. It was how we always greeted each other, but for the first time, I pulled away when I saw Jen and Logan walking toward us. If Aaron noticed, he didn't say anything. I felt mean, but not mean enough to apologize.

"Hey, guys," said Logan.

He lined up to buy tickets for him and Jen, and she grinned over her shoulder at us as though she still couldn't believe she was on a date with the most gorgeous boy in the entire school.

Aaron paid for my ticket, which I thought was sweet. He seemed a little nervous, but probably because of Logan. Until now, it had always been the three of us, and Logan kind of altered the dynamics. We bought popcorn from the vendor and filled into seats somewhere in the middle of the auditorium.

I didn't tell Aaron, but it was the first time I had been to the cinema. My stomach was fluttering, and when the screen came to life and the commercials began to play, I was mesmerized. It was as though the cinema was reconfirming my belief that I belonged in the entertainment industry and that my destiny did not include becoming a pharmacist.

After the movie, we went to the diner for milkshakes. Jen, Aaron, and I chatted non-stop about the film and John Cusack, our favorite flavor shakes, and Logan remained quiet, which I guessed was because the three of us were so comfortable with each other that he probably felt a little left out. He finished his drink quickly and said that he had to shoot off home. I could see that Jen was a little disappointed, but she tried not to show it in front of him, and after he left, she talked about nothing else. She was smitten.

The following week at school, we hardly saw Jen. She sat with Logan in the cafeteria, and she walked home with him after school or stayed behind to watch him at basketball practice. She sat next to him in English and math, and it seemed that whenever I looked at her, she was gazing into his eyes with an expectant smile on her face, like a puppy waiting to be told they've been good.

"Jen has got it bad," Aaron said to me one day as we were walking to class. "I wonder if our boy Logan's going to let her down, though."

"What do you mean?" I asked him.

"Have you not noticed how he's always heading somewhere while Jen follows him? When have you seen him following her, or coming to sit with us in the cafeteria, huh?"

Aaron's words surprised me. I knew exactly what he meant, and of course, he was right. I just hadn't known how to put it into words; aside from Jen and Aaron, my relationship experience was practically zero. I rarely even spoke to my own brother. I didn't even know if Joseph had a girlfriend in college.

"Do you think he doesn't like her that much?" I asked.

"We'll see. I hope he'll prove me wrong, but I have my doubts."

It was all I could think about after that, and I constantly sought them out so that I could see for myself. Aaron was right — Logan barely made any eye contact with Jen, and even when she sat with him at lunch, he spoke more to his friends than he did to her.

I called her over to sit with us, and she just shook her head and smiled at us as if she was happy where she was.

I was conflicted. On the one hand, I wished that Logan wouldn't treat my best friend so badly, but on the other, I understood how she felt. I only wished that she wouldn't be so meek and would stand up for herself a bit more. I'd read enough books to know that if she walked away and came to sit with us, he would take more notice of her absence than her presence, clinging to his elbow.

Logan was playing for the school basketball team one afternoon, and Jen walked home with me and Aaron.

"Do you have another date planned?" I asked her.

She shook her head. "Not yet, but I'm working on it."

"Why are *you* working on it?" asked Aaron. "Shouldn't he be the one to suggest something?"

"That's just it," said Jen. "He hasn't suggested anything yet, and besides, that's so old-fashioned. There's nothing wrong with me asking him to go out with me." She smiled and nudged Aaron with her elbow, but I noticed the way her voice cracked.

On Saturday, I was sweeping up hair from the floor in the salon when Logan walked in. He nodded at me before walking over to Marie, one of the stylists. She stopped trimming a woman's hair when she saw him, slid the scissors and metal comb into a pocket of her tunic, and reached into her trouser pocket for some money, which she handed over to

Logan. He took it and walked out again, giving me a brief nod as he passed.

"Alright there, Jade?" asked Bianca the owner. "You look like you're hugging that broom instead of sweeping with it."

She laughed, and everyone else turned around to stare at me.

I quickly finished what I was doing and asked the customers if they wanted a hot drink so that I could escape to the kitchen. While the kettle boiled, I realized that Marie must be his mom — I could see the resemblance.

I barely spoke to Marie. She was one of those women who non-stop chatted to the customers about their husbands, their kids, their homes, and then when the salon was quiet, sat there with a coffee and a scowl on her face while she flicked through a magazine. It was like she had a customer-face and a resting-face, and the two were entirely different.

When I finished work that evening, Bianca counted out my wages, and I stepped outside. I had walked to the end of the road and turned the corner toward home, when Logan pounced on me, making me jump.

"Logan!" I stepped back. "What are you doing here? Are you meeting your mom?"

He peered over my shoulder exaggeratedly. "No, I'm meeting you." He grinned.

"What… why? I mean, I'm going home."

He checked the time on his watch. "It's early, Jade. It's Saturday. Don't be so boring."

I was confused. "Is Jen with you?"

He peered all around him and even under his arm. "Nope! I don't see her."

"Are you going on a date with her?"

He shook his head, and his expression turned serious. "Look, Jade, that date last week was more of a sorry for spoiling her lunch, and she's a nice girl and all that …"

"But?" I was scared to ask, but at the same time, I knew where this was going.

"But …" He shrugged. "… I'm more interested in you."

"Me?"

My heart was racing, my face felt hot, and I realized I must've looked like such a mess after work and probably smelled of perm solution and hairspray. That was my first thought. My second thought was: what would Jen say?

"Yeah…" He stepped closer and tucked my hair behind my ear. "Don't tell anyone, but that day in the cafeteria, I crashed into Jen deliberately so that I could get to know you."

I blinked, not quite believing what he was saying. This was Logan. This was the boy my best friend had a serious crush on, and he was telling me that he liked me, and not her.

I swallowed. "Why didn't you just talk to me?"

"It's not that easy when you're joined at the hip to your boyfriend."

"My… my boyfriend?" I shook my head.

"Aaron, the kid we went to the cinema with."

He said it like we were the ones who had gone on the date, and Jen and Aaron had tagged along and gotten in the way.

"He's not my boyfriend," I said.

It was the truth. Aaron was *not* my boyfriend, and it wasn't something that either of us had ever discussed or considered during our friendship, and yet I still felt as though I was cheating on him, and my stomach twisted with guilt.

"Great!" Logan rubbed his hands together. "Fancy coming to the diner later, then?"

It still felt like he was messing with me, so I said, "With you?"

"No, with the President, silly! Of course, with me." He was watching me closely, waiting for my response.

I wanted to go, but there was no way my mother would let me go out on a Saturday night, or on a date with boy, and even less chance that she would let me go out on a Saturday night date with a blue-eyed American boy.

And then I remembered Jen.

"I'm sorry, I can't." I shook my head and turned to walk away.

"I won't give up, Jade Xiu," he called after me.

When I glanced over my shoulder, he was gone.

Chapter Fourteen

"Where were you on Saturday?" Aaron asked.

We were approaching the school entrance Monday morning. Jen had dashed off to find Logan when we arrived and was nowhere to be seen.

"Saturday?" I asked. "I was working at the salon."

"I know. I came to meet you when you finished."

"You did?" My thoughts were racing the way they had been racing ever since my encounter with Logan on Saturday, and they were still no closer to settling. Now I was worried that Aaron might have seen us together.

"I was going to take you out to dinner, but they said you'd already left."

He was watching me for a reaction, but I was too busy replaying the scene in my head. I was almost a hundred percent certain no one had seen us.

"Bianca let me go while she finished up," I murmured. "Sorry."

"Maybe next time, yeah? I'll make sure I get there earlier."

I nodded. I wasn't really paying attention because I'd spotted Logan with a couple of his friends, and Jen walking along with them, although none of them were even looking at her. I wished Logan would stop stringing her along and tell her if he didn't want to keep seeing her. Sure, she would be upset, but at least she could stop making herself look like a fool. It was unfair the way he was treating her.

Aaron followed my gaze. "The boy's an asshole. Why doesn't he tell her he doesn't like her?"

We had chemistry first period. Aaron and I always paired up for experiments, and we were reading through the lesson's notes when Logan walked in with his familiar swagger as though he knew the world loved him. I was surprised — I hadn't seen him in chemistry before now.

He paired up with a blonde girl called Melissa, and my cheeks grew hot when I saw the way she gazed at him from beneath her long thick eyelashes.

I kept busy measuring liquids and writing notes, forcing myself not to look at him, although I felt certain that he was staring at me the whole time. Aaron was about to add the final ingredient to our test tube when Logan walked past our station and nudged Aaron's arm, causing him to spill the liquid onto the table and knock over the glass vial. The whole experiment was ruined.

"What the hell?!" shouted Aaron, holding the empty beaker in front of him.

"Sorry, man."

Logan shrugged and wandered back to his desk. Melissa was giggling behind her hand. When she saw me glaring, her face flushed, and she looked away, but Logan simply raised his eyebrows at me as if he was reminding me that he was there.

Aaron was still complaining about the ruined experiment at lunch when Jen came and sat with us.

"What happened?" she asked.

Aaron told her about Logan. "He did it on purpose."

Jen shook her head and popped a cherry tomato into her mouth. It seemed all Jen ever ate these days was salad. "I'm done with him," she mumbled.

"Good!" I said. When she looked at me with her mouth open, I added, "He's been horrible to you, Jen. You deserve someone who's going to treat you better."

Aaron nodded and squeezed her hand as a tear trickled down her face.

"I know," she said. "You're right. I just thought… I dunno… I thought he liked me."

I didn't know what to say. Maybe I should have told her what happened outside the salon, but I had a feeling that would only make things worse, and it was probably better to forget it ever happened.

I didn't know how the boy did it, but it still seemed that every time I glanced around, he was there. I tried closing my mind off to him, pretending he wasn't there, especially as Jen was so quiet now that he hadn't even spoken to her all week. But I couldn't stop my heart from doing this funny little flutter whenever I spotted him out of the corner of my eye. I didn't know what it was about him, but I still couldn't help but think he was the most beautiful boy I had ever seen.

Walking down the school hallway one afternoon, two boys called Aaron over to talk about the upcoming football match. As soon as he told me he'd catch up with me later and walked off, Logan appeared at my side and dragged me into an empty classroom, closing the door behind us.

"What are you doing?" I asked.

"It was the only way to get you alone, Jade," he said, perching on the edge of the teacher's desk and pulling me toward him. "I told you I wasn't giving up."

My heart was skipping around like a lost rabbit, and I felt my cheeks growing hot under his stare. I didn't know what to say, so I kept quiet.

"Go out with me on Saturday," he said.

"I—I can't. I'm working."

"After work, Jade. I'll meet you at the salon."

I wondered what my mother would say if she knew what I was doing right now. I could hear her voice in my head, yelling as she threw my dinner in the trash. "I can't, I'm sorry. I have to go home after."

"It's Saturday evening, Jade. Tell your parents you have a hot date."

"Ha!" I snapped. "They would lock me up if I told them that."

He grinned as if he found it amusing. "Tell them you're working late, or doing something boring like studying, or seeing Aaron."

I winced at the mention of Aaron being boring. Aaron was my friend. Jen was my friend. And Logan had treated neither of them kindly.

I pulled away and shook my head. "Sorry, but I can't." I turned and walked away. And this time when I glanced back, he was smiling at me almost sadly.

If nothing else, Logan was persistent.

He slipped notes into my locker, asking me to meet him at the bleachers, or after school, or early mornings. He turned up when I finished work and walked part of the way home with me, only leaving when I told him my dad knew Karate. He brushed past me in the cafeteria, the feel of his arm against mine making me tingle.

I had never had attention from a boy before. Sure, I'd been friends with Aaron since our first year in high school, but that wasn't the same — we didn't think of each other that way. This was different. I'd watched enough TV programs about teenagers and high school and dating to understand that he liked me, but not enough to figure out how to handle it.

And plus, there was Jen. She still followed him with her eyes everywhere he went, so it was obvious she wasn't over him. Part of me kept thinking that this was my life, and I should do whatever felt right to me, but another part of me was insisting that Jen would never forgive me if she thought that I was seeing Logan.

One Saturday, he was waiting for me outside the salon with a small bundle of random flowers that looked as though they had been picked from the park or someone's front garden.

"For you," he said. "Special flowers for a special girl."

I had already warned my mother that I might have to work a little later, so when he asked me if I wanted to grab a shake with him, I said, "Yes."

It was strange sitting on the same side of a booth with Logan, nothing like sitting opposite from Aaron, whom I felt I knew inside out. Logan and I barely knew each other. He knew nothing about my culture or my family history, and I didn't even know where he lived. He talked about football and basketball, all the stuff that boys talk about when they're with their friends. Eventually, he stopped talking about himself long enough to ask me what I wanted to do after college.

"I want to be a rock star," I said, peering at him over the top of my chocolate shake.

He laughed out loud. "You're kidding, right? What do you *really* want to do?"

It had never sounded lame to me before, but now I felt like a silly little girl who still attended kindergarten, a girl who watched TV shows and imagined herself as the next Madonna.

His smile faded. "You're not kidding? You really want to be a rock star? That's cool, man. Maybe I'll be your manager someday."

Something inside me lit up when he said that. I had always felt as though Aaron and Jen were simply humoring me when I talked about being on stage, but strangely, when Logan reacted this way, it felt as though he was the only person in the world who completely understood me. Maybe I was kidding myself, but I almost pictured my first concert with Logan standing at the side of the stage cheering me on.

He walked me halfway home, and when he stopped me on the sidewalk and kissed me, I closed my eyes and let him.

I didn't tell Jen or Aaron about Logan or the diner or the kiss. The secret burned a hole in my chest but also made me so excited I could barely concentrate on my studies. I grew clumsy, dropping pens in class and mumbling incorrect answers whenever a teacher asked me a question. I felt Logan's eyes on me every minute of the day, even when he wasn't in the same room. I felt different. It was as though the kiss had transformed me from a little girl to a young woman, experiencing all the new emotions that went along with it.

Logan waited for me outside the salon again the following Saturday. This time, instead of heading toward Main Street and the diner, we walked away from town.

"Where are we going?" I asked.

"My parents are both out. I thought we'd go back to my place." He didn't look at me but held onto my hand tightly in case I tried to escape.

I was nervous. The only other house I had ever been in was Jen's, and I felt as comfortable there as I did in my own home, so I didn't know what to expect, and I gasped when I saw the size of the house.

There were wide wrought iron gates at the front of the driveway, which wound through what looked like a mini park to get to the house. The house was huge and white with a porch that ran the whole length of the front façade. Three large shiny cars were parked out the front; I didn't know much about cars, but they certainly looked nothing like my father's beat-up old vehicle.

He followed my gaze. "The silver one is mine."

"Why don't you drive it?" I asked, staring at the car.

"Long story." He let us into the house, and I took my shoes off to leave them by the front door. I noticed he kept his on.

The hallway was as grand as the outside of the house, with a wide galleried staircase directly in front of us, and huge paintings on the walls, which were all pale and creamy like the carpet. Chandeliers hung from the ceiling, almost reaching low enough for me to touch.

"This way," he said. He was already on the bottom stair.

"Where are we going?"

"My room. We can listen to some music. You can show me how well you can sing." He gave a short snappy laugh, which I ignored because I was still too busy taking in my surroundings and breathing in the clean lemony smell of the house.

I followed him upstairs. His room was larger than the whole ground floor of my house, and he had a huge king size bed all to himself. There were posters on the walls of cars, baseball players I didn't recognize, and another of Farrah Fawcett. He slid a CD into the player and filled the room with Bruce Springsteen.

"He's the greatest rock star of all time," he said.

I nodded.

I was still studying Farrah Fawcett's image when his arms slid around my waist from behind, and I felt his breath on my cheek. I jumped and pulled away.

"What are you doing?" I hoped he couldn't see the goosebumps on my arms and the back of my neck.

"What do you think I'm doing, Jade? Come on, don't play innocent with me now."

He grabbed my hands and pulled me close, pressing me against his chest and kissing me hard on the lips. I gave into the kiss. I was breathless, and my thoughts scattered all over the place, but when he started dragging me back toward his bed, I pushed him away.

"I have to go," I said. I couldn't look at him.

"What? Why?" He reached for my arm, and I snatched it away. "What did I do? I thought you wanted to spend time with me."

"I do." I kept my head down. "But… not like this. I can't be here."

I ran down the stairs, collected my shoes from the mat inside the front door, and ran down the driveway, praying his mom wouldn't come home and find me. Who knew what she would think had happened in her son's room?

Monday morning, in school, Logan slipped another note into my locker. I met him at lunch on the bleachers overlooking the football field, making an excuse to Jen and Aaron saying that I had to run over some math homework with the teacher.

He was already waiting when I arrived. I slid onto the bench beside him and waited for him to speak.

"Jade, I'm sorry. I acted like a jerk. I should have asked you if you were comfortable with coming up to my room and… you know… other stuff."

"Yeah, you should," I said. "My parents would kill me if they knew I'd been in your house, let alone in your room."

He looked at me then, his eyes narrowed. "Are they that strict?"

"Uh-huh, especially my mother. She still lives by Chinese rules even though she came here to escape them."

"Okay," he said. "So, what now?"

I stared back at him. "What do you mean, what now?"

"I mean, I like you, Jade. And I thought you liked me, so how do we get around the rules and see each other?"

"See each other?" I was aware that I was repeating everything he said, but this was all new to me, and I didn't know what to think.

"Yeah, like, you know, dates and stuff."

I shook my head and stared out across the field. "I don't know. They won't let me go out in the evenings, and Jen wouldn't like it."

"Why are you thinking about Jen? What does it matter what she thinks? This is your life, Jade. You can't waste it doing what other people tell you to do. Unless I've got it totally wrong, and you don't like me."

"No, I do like you, I do." I hesitated, blushing.

I hadn't meant to blurt it out that way, but now that I'd said it, I realized I'd liked him from the first moment I saw him.

He grinned at me then. "Cool. Look, my parents won't be around this afternoon after school. Why don't you come back to my place again, and we can start over? No pressure, I promise. We'll listen to some Bruce Springsteen, I'll fix you some cookies and milk, and then I'll walk you home. That is, if you can ditch your friends."

It was easy to ditch Jen and Aaron; I told them my mother wanted me to help prepare for the Chinese New Year festival, and that she was refusing to take no for an answer. They knew that since I missed the parade to perform in *West Side Story*, I had not been allowed to forget my disobedience and was still trying to make up for it.

Logan was true to his word. He poured cold milk into tall tumblers, and we ate freshly-baked chocolate chip cookies. I listened to Bruce Springsteen and fell in love with his voice and his lyrics. I helped Logan with his English homework — he was struggling over a *Romeo and Juliet* essay, and he listened to me sing a song from *Grease*, 'Hopelessly Devoted to You' and told me I was better than Olivia Newton-John.

I felt bad making excuses to Jen and Aaron for spending less and less time with them, but I couldn't resist spending time with Logan. He made me smile. He made me feel special. I longed for the day that I could tell everyone that he was my boyfriend and sit with him in the cafeteria the way Britany sat with her boyfriend these days, instead of Laura. I convinced myself that Jen would be okay with it once it was official. I would tell her that nothing happened until long after she stopped seeing him, and that I kept it quiet because I was worried about hurting her feelings.

It didn't occur to me to ask Jen and Aaron what they were up to when I wasn't with them. There wasn't enough room in my head for anyone else apart from Logan.

Logan's parents were going away one weekend, and Logan was planning on having a party. He'd invited lots of people from our year in school, and some friends from his previous school, too. I was invited. I hadn't yet figured out what I was going to tell my parents, but Logan had invited Jen and Aaron, which made me even more excited. Without them there, I thought I would be too nervous to be introduced to Logan's other friends.

A week before the party, I was in the salon, handing out cups of coffee to the customers, when I overheard Logan's mom talking to a woman with lilac hair about him.

"My son has really settled down in his new school. After what happened before, we were worried for a while, you know, when he got involved with the wrong crowd, but now, he's happy. He even mentioned he's been seeing a girl. We've not met her yet, but I know she's good for him because he's been smiling a lot these days."

The customer nodded along while Marie talked, and I pretended that I wasn't listening. In the back room, I couldn't stop myself from smiling. Logan had told his mom about me. She said I was good for him. It was only a matter of time before everyone knew we were dating, and then my parents would have to accept it.

So, when Logan took me back to his house that evening after work, I didn't stop him when he wanted to take things further. This was America. I was a seventeen-year-old girl with a gorgeous American boyfriend. It was about time I started living my life.

Chapter Fifteen

Logan was going to tell everyone about us at the party. I didn't understand why it needed to be so dramatic — and I was the one who loved drama and the stage – but he said it was the way he wanted to do it, to make it more special.

I barely saw him around school during the week leading up to the party. I guessed he was busy making sure everyone was coming, and we were doing practice tests for our final exams, so everyone was feeling the pressure. Jen spent most of her time in the art department — she was worried that her grades weren't good enough to get her into college, and she was working on a series of portraits for her finals. Aaron and I tried to reassure her that she had nothing to worry about, but we barely saw her, either.

"I'll pick you up and take you to the party on Saturday?" Aaron suggested while we were eating our lunches outside under the trees.

It was a lovely day, and we didn't want to waste the sunshine stuck inside the building when everyone was so edgy and anxious during the finals. Aaron had already passed his driver's test, and his parents had bought him an old car; I hadn't even gotten my permit yet.

"Oh… um …"

I didn't know what to say because I hadn't expected this from Aaron. All kinds of thoughts were spinning around inside my head, but I eventually settled for, "I thought I would get ready and go with Jen."

He seemed surprised, his eyebrows almost meeting in the middle. "I think Jen might be going with someone else."

"Someone else?" It was my turn to be surprised. "Who?"

"Jade, have you not noticed that she's been a little... preoccupied recently?" He smiled at me the way a parent would smile at their child when they said something comical.

"She's been worried about her grades," I said.

"We both know that Jen's grades will be on track. You don't think it's something else. A boy, maybe?"

How had I not noticed? I'd been so wrapped up in thoughts of me and Logan that I had not even noticed that my best friend was interested in a boy. Guilt flooded through me, and I felt my cheeks growing hot.

"I... I hadn't thought of that."

"So, what do you think? I'll pick you up at seven. Maybe you'll introduce me to your parents."

I shook my head. I couldn't even picture introducing my parents to Jen, and they would have a fit if they had to meet a boy, even if he was just a friend. Plus, I still hadn't mentioned the party, clothes, or makeup to them, and I had no idea how they were going to react.

"I'm not sure...," I mumbled. "They don't know ..."

Aaron's hand rested on mine. "Jade, I'm sorry, I was messing. I know how it is, and I don't expect to be introduced to your parents. I'll even wait down the road for you, okay? No pressure. Whatever it takes to get you out of the house."

My eyes welled with tears at his kindness and patience. For the first time, I looked at Aaron the way I looked at Logan, but there was something indefinable that was lacking, and he simply didn't measure up.

I took a deep breath as I studied my reflection in the mirror. My parents had never seen me in anything other than the clothes my mother made for me on her little sewing machine, or my pajamas, and I knew they would be shocked because I was wearing my mother's worst nightmare dress.

Jen bought it for me, and it had remained hidden in the bottom of my dresser ever since: a little black silky dress. I curled my hair and was wearing black combat boots that I had bought with the money I earned from the salon. I felt confident. I felt the way I had always longed to feel, the way Jen felt when she looked in the mirror; I felt as though I were making my American girl debut.

My knees were shaking as I walked down the stairs. I took a deep breath before entering the living room and stood inside the doorway, wondering if they could hear my heart thumping.

My mother looked up at me from the armchair and gasped. My father raised his head from the newspaper he was reading, and his mouth opened. He spoke rapidly to my mother in Chinese as though they had forgotten I could understand, "What is she wearing? What is happening?"

"What are you doing?" my mother shrieked. "Where did this dress come from?"

"I'm going to a party, Ma, with my friends."

She shook her head vigorously, my father jabbering away at her.

"Yes, you heard me correctly. I said, with my friends." I kept my voice calm, even despite the turmoil going on inside me. "Everyone from my year will be there, and I will look stupid if I am not allowed to go. You wanted me to be a Chinese American girl, and that's what I am being — going to a party doesn't make me a bad person."

I turned around and walked toward the front door. "Don't wait up for me," I called over my shoulder. *A few more steps*, I thought, *a few more steps, and I'm free.*

"Jade, get back here!" my mother yelled. "Get back here!"

I closed the door softly behind me.

The front door of Logan's house was wide open when we arrived. We could hear the music from the driveway. Aaron parked his car behind the others that were already there, and we made our way inside.

I was so nervous I could barely concentrate on moving one step in front of the other. Aaron held my hand, and we pushed our way through the kids mingling in the entrance hallway and through to the kitchen, where there were bottles on every surface.

"What do you want to drink?" Aaron asked me.

"Huh? Just a soda, thank you."

I was looking for Logan. He wasn't in the kitchen, but I could see lots of kids in the back garden already, so when Aaron handed me a soda, I suggested we go outside.

"Don't look so nervous, Jade," he said. "Enjoy it. This will be the first of many once we get to college." He raised his soda to mine, and we toasted each other.

I couldn't find Logan in the garden, either.

"Have you seen Jen yet?" asked Aaron.

I shook my head. Where was Logan? In my mind, I had pictured him waiting with open arms for me to arrive, excited to announce that I was his girlfriend. I could still feel his hands on me from last weekend, still taste him on my lips, still blush whenever I remembered that he had seen me naked. A thought suddenly occurred to me that Logan might have told his friends what we did, and I glanced around at them to see if anyone was pointing at me and snickering, but they were all laughing and chatting and drinking beer.

"Okay?" Aaron smiled at me, a look of concern on his face.

I smiled back. "It's just all… new, I guess," I said.

We stayed in the garden for a while, listening to music and chatting the way we always chatted. Aaron and I knew each other better than anyone else ever would. Gradually, I allowed myself to relax. Logan would appear when he was ready, and then everyone would know about us.

As the sun sank lower in the sky, and the night turned purple. Everyone drifted back inside the house. We followed. The music was blaring in the living room, and there were kids everywhere, sprawled on sofas, boys with their arms around girls, leaning against the wall with a can or a plastic cup in their hand. Some people were dancing in the middle of the room, arms raised above their heads.

I felt the music surging through my veins and making me feel alive.

"Shall we dance?" I asked Aaron.

Logan wouldn't mind. He knew that we were friends, and he would want me to be enjoying the party instead of being a wallflower.

We were full-on crazy dancing to Michael Jackson's 'Beat It' when Logan finally entered the room, his arm around another girl. The music faded behind the pounding in my ears, my stomach lurching and heaving. As the girl turned around, he lowered his head and kissed her on the lips. It was Jen.

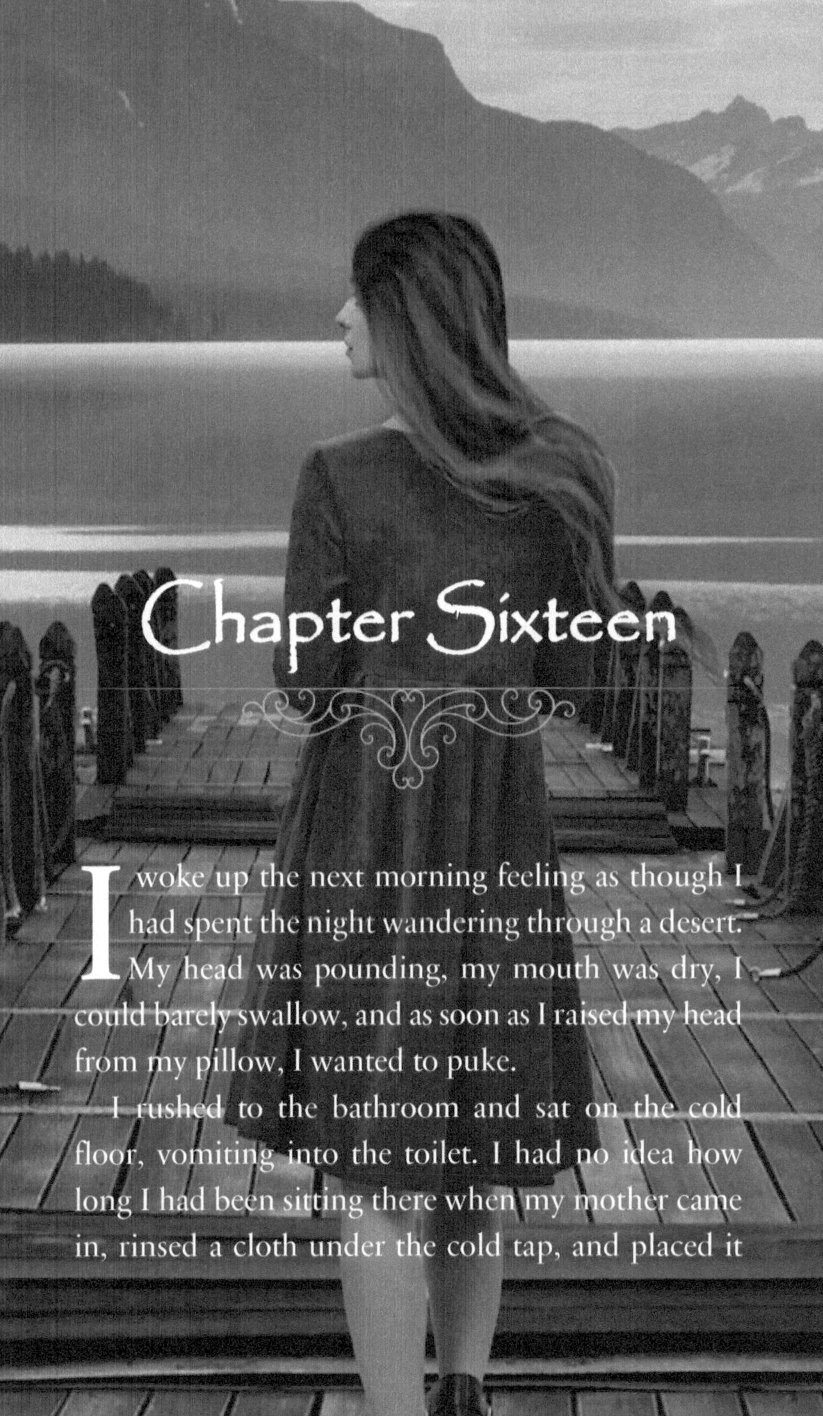

Chapter Sixteen

I woke up the next morning feeling as though I had spent the night wandering through a desert. My head was pounding, my mouth was dry, I could barely swallow, and as soon as I raised my head from my pillow, I wanted to puke.

I rushed to the bathroom and sat on the cold floor, vomiting into the toilet. I had no idea how long I had been sitting there when my mother came in, rinsed a cloth under the cold tap, and placed it across my forehead. She didn't speak, and I barely opened my eyes to look at her.

The last thing I remembered from the party was asking Aaron to pour me another drink, and when he refused, I poured myself a drink, egged on by one of Logan's friends.

"Drink, it! Drink it! Drink it!" he chanted while some other boys joined in.

I vaguely recalled Jen's perfectly painted lips saying, "Jade? Are you drunk?" and then voices in the background.

Aaron murmuring, "It's okay, I'll take her home."

And then nothing.

I spent the day in bed forcing my brain to remain empty and sick. If I was sick forever, I might never have to go back to school and face anyone. I didn't need to go to college to be a rock star. I didn't need a master's in chemistry, or biology, or anything else for that matter. I could work with my mom until I found a band to join, and no one would ever need to know.

It was the humiliation that stopped my body from working. If Logan had liked Jen all along, why did he keep pursuing me? I was so confused. I was too sick to work it all out.

That evening, my mother brought a bowl of steamed rice and vegetables into my bedroom and made me sit up while she propped my pillows behind my head. She sat on the edge of the bed and fed me in silence. I was grateful that she wasn't asking questions.

The following morning, my mother didn't go to work. She came into my room and shook me awake.

"Time to get up for school, Jade," she said.

I peered at her with dry eyes. My head had stopped pounding, and the memory of Jen and Logan had come rushing back, but I no longer felt sick.

"I can't go," I mumbled. "I'm still sick."

"You are going," she said, dragging the covers off my shivering body. "You get drunk; you suffer consequences."

"I've never missed a day of school," I whined. "One day won't hurt." I never told her that I had no intention of going back, ever.

She grabbed my arm and pulled me out of bed. "Wash your face. You feel better. I take you to school."

As if I hadn't suffered enough humiliation, I couldn't arrive to school with my mother. Everyone would laugh at me.

"Alright, alright," I said. "I'm getting up."

I left home without eating breakfast, snuck into school early, and changed into my real-Jade clothes in the bathroom. I kept my head down in homeroom and headed to math, sliding into a seat at the back of the class.

Within seconds, Aaron slid into the seat beside me. "Jade, are you okay?" he whispered, his face close to mine.

I nodded. "I'm fine."

"What did your parents say? Were you in trouble?"

"Nothing; they didn't say anything."

"They seemed really nice when I dropped you off. Your mom was worried about you. I mean, you couldn't even stand up straight."

"You met my parents?" I stared at him, waiting for him to tell me he was joking, but his expression remained concerned.

"Uh-huh, someone had to make sure that you got home okay."

"Thank you," I mumbled, reaching into my bag for my textbook.

Aaron took me home, and my mother had not even mentioned it. She must be saving her anger for tonight. Maybe that was why she didn't go to work today, because she needed to figure out my punishment before I got home.

Logan strolled into the room, his arm around Jen, who saw us and gave a little wave.

"Are you okay?" she whispered.

I nodded and removed my pencil, ruler, and compass from my math set. I couldn't sit here knowing that they were sitting a few seats away, together, boyfriend and girlfriend. I couldn't even face Logan. I sensed Aaron shrugging at Jen in response to a silent question and stared out of the window, blinking back tears.

I should've been worried that my best friend was seeing a boy who was cheating on her with me. But at the same time, he was cheating on me with her. Maybe I should've warned her not to trust him. But I was so consumed by anger and humiliation that I could think about nothing else but running out of the building and never coming back.

I wished my parents had never come to America. My father should've just lived in China with my mother. I wished they had let me be a normal girl who understood boys and knew how to behave in a normal relationship. I wished I had a mother who had explained to me about growing up, and sex, and emotions, and taught me how to know when people were genuine and when people were using me.

I blamed them completely.

It didn't occur to me that Jen was a normal girl, and yet Logan was using her, too. All I knew was that he didn't want me; he never wanted me, and I still wanted him.

"Jade?" Aaron's voice penetrated my thoughts. "Stop!" He reached for my hand and held it tightly.

I tried to snatch it away, but it was slippery, and his grip was so tight, and there was red liquid all over my book. I stared at the red droplets. I glanced at the ceiling to see where it was coming from, but Aaron had raised my hand above my head, and he was saying to the teacher, "Sir, Jade's bleeding. I think I should take her to the nurse."

He helped me to my feet and maneuvered me around the desks, not letting go of my hand. He sat in the medical room while the nurse cleaned my hand and wrapped it with a band-aid. After, instead of returning to class, he took me to the library and sat at a table with me.

"What's going on, Jade?" he asked. "Why did you do that?"

I stared at my hand, and then at Aaron. "Do what?"

"You stabbed your hand with the compass. It was freaky, man. I mean, you didn't even flinch."

I shrugged. I didn't even remember doing it, but now that I thought about it, I could feel the metal point piercing my skin, feel the way it throbbed, drawing my attention away from the pain in my heart and into the wound on my finger.

"So?" Aaron was still staring at me.

"So, what?"

"Are you going to tell me why you did it?"

"I don't know," I said. "But don't worry about it, Aaron. I'm okay."

It wasn't a conscious effort to cause myself pain. My heart was sore. Whenever I saw Jen and Logan together, his arm around her shoulders and squeezing her against his side as if he was scared to let her go, a little bit of me chipped away, and pain was the only way to bring myself back. It was my final year of high school and without the pain, I knew I would never achieve the grades I needed.

A week after the party, and a few days after I cut myself with the compass, I was slicing onions in the kitchen at home when the knife slipped and sliced open the skin on my index finger. It stung like crazy. I rinsed the blood away under the cold tap, wrapped a band-aid around my finger, and realized that for a few minutes, I had completely forgotten about Logan and Jen.

I hid the knife in my room. My mother searched the kitchen, complaining to my father about the missing knife. She asked me if I had seen it, and I said, "No, Ma."

I heard her telling my father that she must have accidentally thrown it away with the trash, and he told her to buy a new one from the hardware store.

That night, before I went to sleep, I sliced the skin on the inside of my thigh. It was tender. I cleaned the wound and lied awake in bed, feeling the way it stung every time I moved. I felt it in school the next day, rubbing against my jeans. It helped me focus. Each time I saw Logan and Jen, I moved my leg and remembered the cut in my flesh, and I was able to push them from my mind.

Jen spent all her time with Logan. Aaron still walked to class with me and still ate lunch with me in the cafeteria, but looking back, I don't recall any of our conversations. I was going through the motions of studying, eating, functioning like a normal teenage girl, until I was alone in my room late at night, and the pain reminded me that I was still alive. If Jen noticed the difference in me, she never mentioned it.

Logan never spoke to me again.

My mother tried speaking to me about the night of the party. She wanted to know why I got drunk, why a boy had brought me home, who else I had secretly been friends with. I kept my answers vague. I told her someone had given me alcohol without me realizing, and that I would be more careful in future.

And all the while, I was planning on getting as far away from them, from school, from everyone I knew, so that I could start my life over again at college. Each night, when I held the knife in my hand, I promised myself that when I got to college, it would all stop. I would be a chrysalis, and at college, I would emerge as a butterfly.

I got accepted into UPenn, but turned it down to go to Lehigh, all just to get further away from my mother.

Lehigh was where Jade Xiu was going to become a rock star.

Struggle Between Two Lives

Chapter Seventeen

Aaron got into Lehigh, too. He wanted to concentrate on getting into the football team, but we both enrolled in the same music course and threw ourselves into every club and activity we could find. I joined an A Capella group. It wasn't what I wanted to sing, but I believed that the more I sang, the sooner I would get noticed, and maybe even get signed by a record label. I was more determined than ever that I was going to be a rock star.

Because I still didn't have the courage to wholly defy my parents, I was studying chemistry as well; they didn't know about the music or my love of singing, and I woke up every morning to lyrics in my head, which only confirmed that if they loved me the way parents should, they would know about my passion.

Wouldn't they? They should be supporting my decisions, encouraging me to grow and to be happy, instead of forcing me into the future they envisaged for me.

It still hadn't occurred to me that my love of music and my determination to be a star might be an act of rebellion. Music was in my blood and in my heart, and I would do anything to follow my dream.

Or so I thought.

My parents drove me to college that first day. They insisted. My mother brought a cooler filled with Chinese food because she was worried that I would eat unhealthily as soon as I was away from my home environment. What she really meant was that she thought I would eat like other Americans. I never heard her question Joseph about his eating habits whenever he came home from Villanova; he still played football, and his physique remained solid and toned, so if he lived on burgers and shakes, it didn't show.

My roommate was already in the room when we arrived. She was also a Chinese American girl named Lana. I could see the relief on my mother's face when she saw Lana, the smile quickly forming as she stepped forward to shake her hand.

Lana, who was on her bed, pillows propped up behind her, reading *The Bell Jar*, folded the book, and returned the smile.

"Hello, Ma," she said politely.

"I am so happy my daughter will be staying with you," my mother said. "What are you studying?"

I groaned inwardly. To my mother, the question was all important, as though the college major defined the person in front of her, and I wished with all my heart that she would learn to accept people for who they were and not for their career choices, or the choices they may have been forced into.

"Science, Ma," the girl replied, her gaze flitting between my mother and me.

My embarrassment faded a little. I could tell that Lana understood how forceful my parents were because she had been brought up the same way — why else would she be studying science when there were so many other options? I hoped that we would become good friends.

Since Jen became Logan's girlfriend, we had drifted apart. Jen wanted to spend all her time with him, and when she wasn't with him, I made excuses not to see her. If she was hurt by my behavior, she didn't say so, but a couple of times, I had caught her speaking quietly with Aaron and glancing away whenever she caught sight of me.

My mother reached into the cooler, muttering in her broken English, that she had brought sweet treats as a welcome gift for my roommate. She handed her a plastic tub of food.

"Welcome," she said, as though Lana had come to stay in our home, rather than the two of us being allocated this square room with two beds, two desks, and a *Starsky and Hutch* poster, which I assumed my roommate had brought with her.

"Thank you, Ma," Lana said, inclining her head respectfully.

In Chinese, my mother said to me, "You see what a good Chinese American girl you will be sharing room with," as though she thought Lana would not understand her words.

I felt heat rising in my cheeks. I wished they would leave, but instead, my father stared out of the window, and my mother unpacked my stuff, unfolding clothes and refolding them in exactly the same way, smoothing them with the palms of her hands and patting them like they were puppies.

I sat on the end of the bed, praying that they would leave so that I could be free of them, released from the Asian parameters they had placed around my life the moment I was born, giving me no choice but to fit their mold.

When my clothes were finally unpacked and placed neatly inside the two bottom drawers allocated to me, my books and writing materials spread neatly across the desk, my mother stopped in the middle of the room, picking at her fingers as though she didn't know what to do with her hands. My father turned away from the window and looked at me for the first time since we arrived.

"I'll be fine, Ma," I said.

I didn't feel fine, but I brushed it aside so they'd drive away and leave me here to begin the next chapter of my life. I felt the fresh wounds on my thighs opening up and growing wet with blood, and I focused on them, on the way they rubbed against the cloth of my pants. A few more minutes, and they would be gone, and I could settle into my new life.

My mother nodded, a brief jerky movement, and I held my breath, hoping she wouldn't try to hug me. My father checked his watch and met my eyes, an action so out of character that I couldn't look away.

"Yù," he said. "You're a good girl."

Then he turned and left the room, but not before I noticed the tears in his eyes.

My mother followed him with her eyes. She gave a long last look around the room that would be her daughter's new home. It felt as though she wanted to say something, and I allowed myself to hope that she would tell me to be happy, to enjoy college, to follow my dreams.

"Be good, Jade," she said instead. And then they were gone.

I glanced at Lana, whose head was already buried back in the pages of her book.

"Sorry," I said.

I had never apologized for my parents before, but it was probably because they had never been introduced to any of my friends before. I wondered if they assumed that Lana and I would simply share a room, sleeping in beds that had been slept in by countless other teenagers like me, facing our respective walls, maybe only speaking about our classes, our essays, studying, and research, like good Chinese American girls.

"My parents are the same," she said.

I looked at Lana, at her eyes, which were lined with thick black kohl, perfect flicks in each corner, at her pierced ears, and the red stripes dyed into her hair. She had a *Starsky and Hutch* poster. She wore jeans with red Doc Marten boots and a red silky top, which slipped off one shoulder. She must have changed her clothes as soon as her parents left campus.

"Did they make you bring dumplings?"

She reached beneath her bed, dragged out a plastic box, and opened the lid to reveal a small mountain of food in Tupperware tubs. "Uh-huh."

I laughed. I already liked Lana. "Do they know you wear these clothes?"

"Yes."

I blinked furiously, mouth open. "And they let you?"

"They knew they had no choice. I'd have dressed the way I wanted to dress whether they liked it or not, and my mother said no daughter of hers was sneaking about changing in the school toilets where anyone could see her naked butt."

"She said that?"

"Not in so many words, no."

Lana was funny despite the fact that she didn't smile much. She made me laugh though, made me feel more comfortable in the first five minutes of getting to know her than I'd felt during the whole last year of high school.

"Do your parents want you to be a doctor?"

"Brain surgeon, dentist, shrink. Anything that means I have to poke about inside people's heads. I told them I'd like to be a waitress or a flight attendant, you know, see a bit of the world, and they said they'd settle for anything that means I don't have to rely on tips to survive."

"They just took it? They didn't threaten to disown you if your grades were anything less than brilliant?"

"To be fair, my grades are pretty good, so I've not let them down yet, but I think they'll be cool with it so long as I turn up for Chinese New Year and remember how to cook noodles. How about you? You look like you've swallowed the good girl pie and not had the talk yet."

"The talk?"

"Yeah, you know. This is America, Ma. You came here to get away from the constraints of China, so why are you dumping them on my shoulders still? They all try it, you know; it's like they wanted to find their freedom," — she made speech marks in the air around the word – "but once they found it, they didn't know how to handle it. But that's not our problem. It's theirs."

I sat heavily on my bed without moving. When I walked in and saw Lana, I'd felt a wave of disappointment that she was Chinese American, like I'd wanted to forget my culture now that I'd finally escaped home, not be reminded of it every day. But now, I was grateful to have been allocated this roommate — I was going to learn so much from her. Maybe even find the courage to tell my parents what I really wanted to do with my life.

"I want to be a rock star," I blurted out.

She watched me, her eyes scanning my face as if she was trying to work out if I was joking or not.

"Cool." She shrugged. "You haven't told them though, have you?"

"No. I can't even wear normal clothes; Ma has to make them for me on her little sewing machine."

Lana laughed out loud. "I bet dating is out of the question, too."

"I did date a boy, kind of, for a while."

I told her about Logan, how he had pursued me after work and in school, leaving out the part where we had sex. I hadn't told anyone about that and, although it was burning a hole in me that I couldn't assuage, I still couldn't bring myself to say the words. I felt ashamed, I guessed, not because of what we did, but because I was sucked in by Logan's lies. I was embarrassed by my own naivety.

Lana told me about her boyfriend, John. He had gotten a scholarship into a different college. She said they'd planned to see each other at Thanksgiving when they would both be returning home, but she didn't want to settle down with him or anything. She was so calm when she spoke about him, so unaffected by their relationship, the distance between them, the uncertainty of their future, that I was mesmerized listening to her talk.

"Do your parents know about him?" I asked.

"Uh-huh. They know it won't last now that I'm in college, so they didn't try to make me end it. They think it will run its course and come to a natural end without their interference."

"My mother told me not to even bother making friends in school because they would distract me from my studies."

I hoped my jealousy didn't show. Why did I end up with the only parents in America who couldn't trust their daughter to have friends and still get good grades?

"That sucks," said Lana. She returned to her book.

I tidied up the books on my desk and studied my schedule. I had classes with Aaron pretty much every day, and I realized how much I was looking forward to seeing him. He was a reminder that I wasn't entirely alone here in this strange place, and that even if I found it difficult to make friends with anyone else apart from Lana, at least I had Aaron to talk to.

Lana glanced up. "A friend of mine said there's a welcome party tonight by the river. You wanna come? There'll be booze."

"A welcome party? Is that allowed?"

"Not by the teachers, although I bet they'd grab a beer if they happened to pass by. It's a student thing. It'll be fun."

I nodded.

I was in college. It was a new start. I was going to leave Yù behind for good and allow Jade Xiu to shine.

Chapter Eighteen

I expected the welcome party to be like the summer camp farewell party, all grilled sausages and sodas and rope swings. But it wasn't. We were like kids slotted inside adult bodies and left to our own devices with all the freedom grownups took for granted, and we were still learning to adapt.

Music was blaring from large speakers. Some kids were dancing, bottles of beer in their hands, their heads nodding along to the beat. Others were spread out on the grass, relaxing, chatting, laughing.

Groups of kids played cards for money on the grass. Some were kicking a ball around. I felt like a child walking into a candy store with some pocket money, not knowing which way to turn first.

"Let's go grab a beer," suggested Lana.

I followed her to where some boys had stashed a mountain of bottles, and we each took one. Lana wandered around as if it was the most natural thing in the world to be here with a group of new students all prepared to get to know each other. She smiled at everyone, said hi to anyone who acknowledged her, and casually sat on the grass with a group of kids who shuffled around to make room for her.

I felt awkward standing there. I didn't know what to do with my free hand, so I shoved it into my pocket; I didn't know where to look either, so I stared at the hills in the distance beyond the valley as though I were planning a hike in my free time. In my peripheral vision, I saw Lana tip her head back and laugh out loud at something her neighbor had said. I'd kind of hoped she would introduce me to the others, but I guessed we were only roommates, and she wasn't responsible for me.

Maybe I'd already bored her to tears with complaints about my parents. I wished I'd kept quiet. It probably took her about five minutes to work out that I was naïve and clueless when it came to real life and grown-up relationships.

I turned away so that she wouldn't think I was waiting for her to include me in whatever conversation was going on in the circle. I was at college. It was time I learned to make my own friends without waiting for introductions or for them to come to me, because when I thought about it, the few friendships I'd formed at school, I'd literally had zero input. Jen, Britany and Laura, Aaron, and even Logan — they had all found me.

I swallowed a mouthful of beer and blinked as the bubbles escaped up my nose and caused my eyes to water. Blinking, I contemplated heading back to our dorm room and burying my nose in a book. I had no idea how to make friends, and standing here alone while kids all around me were huddled together in groups, or pairs, was making me feel more ridiculous than I'd ever felt before.

I stared at the grass at my feet and tried to convince myself that if six-year-old Jade could do it, seventeen-year-old me had nothing to fear. What was I even afraid of? My fear wasn't a tangible thing that I could show someone, or even something that I could put easily into words, but somewhere along the line, after what happened with Logan, my self-esteem had slipped through my pores and evaporated into the night.

It wasn't until I was standing there alone at the campus welcome party, surrounded by smiling faces and buzzing conversation, that I finally acknowledged that I'd lost the vital part of me that was determined to fit in.

And I didn't know how to get it back.

I was about to walk back to the dorm when warm hands clamped heavily on my shoulders from behind. I jumped and turned around to find Aaron grinning at me.

"Aaron!" I was so grateful to see him that I almost threw my arms around his neck and kissed him but stopped myself in time. "I didn't know you were coming."

"Why wouldn't I? Everyone else is here." He glanced around, taking it all in, his gaze finally settling on the boy he'd arrived with. I followed his gaze. "Jade, this is Sam, my roommate. Sam — Jade."

Sam held out a hand, and as I went to shake it, he pulled me into a tight bearhug.

"Got ya," he said, releasing me.

Sam was tall, his shoulders broad, a footballer probably. His hair was brown, like mine, with a kink in it that curled around his ears and almost over his eyes, and I thought that I had never seen anyone so beautiful in my life.

He smiled at me lazily and said, "Catch ya later. My cousin is over there."

He walked away from us, my eyes glued to his back, the feel of his arms still wrapped around me.

"Is your roommate here?" Aaron asked.

"What?" I turned to Aaron as if he'd suddenly appeared from nowhere. "My roommate? Oh, yes, she's over there on the grass." I pointed out Lana to him, my eyes sliding surreptitiously back to where Sam was standing with a group of other boys all as tall and as wide-chested as he was.

"Are you as nervous as I am?" Aaron asked.

I snapped my attention back to him. "You're nervous? Why?"

He shrugged. "I dunno, it's different, I suppose. There are so many kids here, and it's like they expect us to arrive here in our parents' cars and suddenly understand what it takes to survive alone."

I studied Aaron's face. We'd been friends for years, and if I was honest, I felt closer to Aaron now than I did to Jen, and yet I hadn't realized how blue his eyes were, how straight his teeth were when he smiled, or that he was anxious about coming to college. How had I not known this?

I handed him the bottle of beer that was growing warm in my hand and watched him take a hungry swig.

Chapter Nineteen

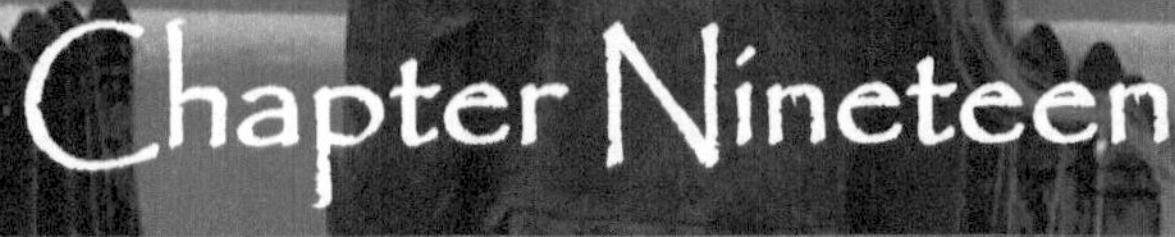

Lana and I were different in so many ways. She would leave her laundry on the floor, on her bed, her socks hung across the headboard, and jeans clinging to the end of her duvet. One afternoon, I returned from class to find her bra peeping out from beneath my pillow. I was still standing in the middle of the room, trying to figure out how it got there, when she came in.

"Hey, Jade," she said. Her gaze took in the garment in my hand, and she smiled as she took it from me. "You found it. I searched everywhere this morning after you left. Where was it?"

"Under my pillow?"

"How did it get there?"

"Well, I didn't put it there," I said.

Glancing around the room, Lana's stuff was everywhere. She had half-open bottles of nail polish lined up along the windowsill. Her hairbrush, knotted with long strands of black hair, laid on the floor beside three left shoes and a screwed-up pair of ripped jeans. Her textbooks took up whatever space remained under the bed, alongside the empty and unwashed Tupperware tubs that she had arrived with, once filled with Chinese food.

My clothes were folded neatly inside the small drawers allocated to me, my books piled on top of the desk in size order, my pens stowed inside a small jar with yellow daffodils painted around the side from an old art project I did at school. My makeup was all inside my makeup bag, which was tucked inside the drawer harboring my pajamas and underwear.

Lana laughed. "You look like my mom standing there checking out the mess."

I sat on the end of my bed and wrenched my eyes away from a pair of jeans I'd spotted stuffed inside a sneaker. I didn't understand how she could live like this.

"Sorry," I said.

I tugged my schedule from my bag and checked out the date my science assignment had to be in.

"I'll clean it up," said Lana.

She wriggled out of her top, her hair mushed up around her face, and dragged another T-shirt over her head. Dropping to her knees, she reached under the bed for a pair of matching sneakers.

"It's under your desk," I said.

She grinned at me. "Thanks."

"Where are you going?"

"A group of us are going into town to grab a burger. Coming?" She slipped her feet into her sneakers and was already heading for the door.

I pictured the diner to be the same as the diner back home, red plastic seats in wide booths, tissues stuffed into a tin can on each table, the ketchup bottles sticky around the lid. It was easier than remembering going to the diner with Logan.

I swallowed. "No… thank you."

"Another time then." The door closed behind her.

I watched Lana cross the campus, saw her wave to a couple of girls I'd seen her hanging around with in the cafeteria when I was with Aaron, and disappear behind the library. As soon as I was certain she wasn't coming back for something she'd forgotten, I found the compass at the bottom of my backpack, unzipped my jeans, laying them neatly on the end of the bed, and pricked the flesh at the top of my thigh with the metal tip.

When I was finished, I held a wad of tissue paper against my skin until the bleeding slowed. For a few moments, I felt like I was outside of my body, floating beneath the ceiling and looking down at my own face with my eyes closed. I looked peaceful, I told myself. Relaxed. In control. It wouldn't always be this way. Soon, I would make friends. I wouldn't be so dependent on Aaron to be seen with me so that I didn't look like the lonely Asian girl who did nothing but study. I would be more like Lana.

My eyes flew open as I remembered the mess strewn around the room. I thought about my bedroom at home, the faded floral bedspread that kept me warm, the clean clothes which my mom returned daily to my room, smelling of lavender and the talcum powder she kept in the bathroom, my desk which was empty of books now that I was no longer there.

Sliding my legs carefully over the side of the bed, I bent to check that I hadn't opened the fresh wound and made it bleed again. It was already starting to scab over, tiny pinpricks of brownish blood crusting over the bobbly surface.

Starting with the stuff under Lana's bed, I retrieved her clothes and sorted them into two piles: dirty and clean. I lined her shoes up in pairs under the bed. I rinsed the containers in the bathroom and stacked them neatly inside each other to save space. I screwed the lids back onto the bottles of nail polish and put them back on the windowsill in color order, dark to light, and pulled the loose hairs from her hairbrush. Then I stacked the books on top of her desk and placed the pens beside them so that they would not roll over the edge and back onto the floor.

I felt better when the room was tidy, like I could concentrate on my assignment without the clutter screaming at me to be tidied away.

It was dark when I turned off my desk lamp and climbed into bed. Lana was still not back from the diner, and I was disappointed that she wouldn't see how tidy our room was until the following morning when it was daylight again. I closed my eyes, and my mind was filled with a vision of my mom telling me what a good Chinese daughter I was keeping the house so clean.

I heard Lana's key scraping against the lock on the outside of the door. It sounded louder than it actually was in the dense darkness, and I sat upright in bed, my heart racing. There was a giggle outside, voices, and I strained to hear what was going on. Maybe it wasn't Lana. Maybe someone was trying to break into our room.

I stared at her bed with the duvet smoothed up to the pillows, which I'd plumped up earlier against the headboard. She wasn't in bed. There was a thump against the door, which resounded inside my head, and a voice said, "Shh," in an urgent whisper.

Without thinking, I jumped out of bed, crossed the room, and pulled the door open. Lana was standing there in the hallway, the key raised to her face as though she were trying to work out what was wrong with it, and behind her, a tall boy with brown curly hair, one arm wrapped around her chest and clearly holding her up.

Sam.

"Aaron's friend," he said when he saw me standing there in the doorway in my pajamas.

"Jade," said Lana. She was squinting at me in the dark, trying to bring me into focus. "Shh, it's late," she whispered to me.

I could smell alcohol on their breath, and it made me want to gag, remembering the time I got drunk at Logan's party.

"Is she drunk?" I asked Sam.

"No," he said. "We're underage, don't you know?"

Lana leaned back against him, and he swayed slightly with her weight. Sam eyed me up and down, and I straightened my top around me, suddenly conscious that I was naked beneath the thin material.

"I think you should go," I said.

He nodded and straightened as though trying to prove that he hadn't been drinking.

"You're right, Aaron's friend. I should go." He propped Lana up against the doorframe, and I caught her as she weaved through the doorway. "Farewell, fair ladies," said Sam, saluting us as he wandered down the hallway toward the stairs.

He began singing a song I didn't recognize and disappeared through the door when he reached the end.

I half-carried Lana into the room and sat her down on her bed, where she flopped heavily back against the pillows.

"I love you, Jade," she said. "You're so… clean."

The next time they went into town, I went with them. Aaron walked with me. Sam had a truck which Lana and a few others had caught a ride in, but there wasn't room for all of us. When we arrived at the diner, there was already a crowd of kids crammed into two booths.

Sam rose when he saw us and gestured for me to slide into the booth where he sat beside me without waiting for Aaron to join us. Aaron grinned and took a spare seat opposite us and next to Lana, who glanced up from the menu and gave him a brief nod.

"I'm glad you came," she said to me with a wink. "It'll do you good to get your head out of your science books."

"Oh, Jade," said Sam, "no one likes a geek. You need to lighten up a bit."

He smiled at me, and I kept my eyes on the menu, hoping he wouldn't notice my burning cheeks.

The diner was noisy — it seemed that it was the place all the students came to, and I felt as though everyone had kind of left me behind because I hadn't known about it. I soaked up the sounds, ate my food, and drank a milkshake, but I was too distracted by Sam's presence beside me to actively take part in any conversation.

Sam was loud without raising his voice. He was lively without leaving his seat. His hair moved around his face, his eyes were everywhere, and I couldn't tell if I was being paranoid, but as the evening progressed, his thigh pressed harder against mine, and whenever he reached for something across the table, his arm brushed against my breast.

I glanced at Aaron from beneath my lashes, and he was oblivious, or at least if he wasn't, he was doing a good job of hiding it. A boy walked in who Aaron knew, and he jumped up and led him to us, telling me, "This guy has a band."

"Whoa, what's that all about?" Sam asked me, his voice managing to sneak beneath the other noisier conversations. "What's this about a band?"

I smiled at him. "I want to be a rock star."

It was the first thing I ever told him about myself.

Chapter Twenty

Lana and I settled into a pattern: I kept the room clean and tidy, and she invited me along whenever there was something sociable going on outside of campus. I gave up expecting her to pick up her laundry, and once a week, I would return with two bags filled with clean clothes: one for me, and one for Lana. If I found a dirty sock draped across my pencil jar, I no longer squirmed.

My mother would have gone crazy if she knew that this was what college life entailed, especially as she'd been so grateful that her daughter was sharing a room with a good Chinese American girl. She wrote to me every week, and I slipped her letters, unread, into my desk drawer.

Lana also listened to me sing. She passed the gym one day when we were practicing A Capella, and that evening, while I was working on an essay, she said, "I heard you today, Jade. You can actually sing."

I stopped writing. She was on her bed, back resting against the pillows, and had already returned to her book, but I felt a glow inside at her comment. Lots of people wanted to become rock stars, I knew that, but very few people made it because very few people were determined. I was one of those determined people.

I'd stepped onto this path when I was a little girl; it was like my yellow brick road, only at the end of it, I wasn't going home. I was going to fly far away and make a life for myself, where I could forget all about where I came from. I was going to be the Jade Xiu the whole world would never forget.

Aaron's friend Gabe, the boy from the diner, played electric guitar. He was mad into Jimi Hendrix and Eric Clapton, which were not the kind of music

I'd ever been interested in, but he had big ideas, according to Aaron. Whenever we came out of music class, he would tell me all about Gabe's band. He didn't have a name for it yet, but he was working on it. He'd found a drummer and a second guitarist, and was looking for songwriters.

"I think we should write a song," said Aaron one day as we were heading to the cafeteria.

"A song? I don't know how to write a song."

Aaron looked puzzled. "You can sing. You know the kind of song lyrics you like. Surely, you've thought about writing your own stuff."

I had thought about it. Now that Aaron mentioned it, I realized that it might have always been loitering in the back of my mind, but I'd never really given it any attention.

"We can do this," he said, finding an empty table. "You can do this."

But I wasn't listening. Sam had walked in with his arm around a pretty blonde girl, and as I watched, he bent down and kissed the top of her head, almost in slow motion, catching my eye as he did so and winking at me.

Lana was writing an essay when I told her that Aaron and I were going to write a song. For someone who spent all her free time off campus and mostly coming home drunk, she never missed a deadline, and she said her grades were still top notch. She stopped writing and put down her pen.

"What kind of song?" she asked eventually.

I shrugged. "I don't know."

"Well, that could be a problem." She turned around and picked up her pen.

"Why?" I asked.

She sighed. "Think of your favorite lyrics, Jade. What is it that you love about them? They must touch something inside you for them to resonate."

"Okay…"

I waited for her to elaborate. It sounded to me as though she didn't think I could do this, and part of me was seething inside and wanting to prove her wrong, but the other part of me was scared that she might be right.

She turned to face me. "Look, I'm no expert, but I don't think writing a song is easy. It has to come from the heart, and I don't think you have enough life experience to know what's inside there yet. Aaron shouldn't be giving you these crazy ideas if they're going to knock you back."

I sat heavily on my bed. I already felt like she'd delivered a blow to my stomach, and I knew she was only trying to help.

"What kind of experience?" I asked.

"Relationships. Love. Broken hearts. Freedom. Travel. There's a whole world out there that you know nothing about."

I chewed my bottom lip. I didn't think Lana knew much more about the world than I did, but even I could see that she had carved a niche for herself in the school's social circle, while I was sitting in our room keeping everything tidy.

"I mean, I bet you've never been skinny-dipping, have you?"

"Skinny-dipping?"

"Yeah, you know, swimming naked. Alright, so it's only one silly small suggestion among a million others, but it would give you a new experience."

I thought about it. I imagined what my mother would say if she knew — she would go ballistic at the thought of other people seeing her daughter naked, at her daughter's body being exposed to the world. I recalled the way she would turn away when I was a child getting undressed to take a bath. If anything would make me want to do this, it was the knowledge that my mother would hate it. This was America. This was the land of freedom.

"Sure." I nodded. "We should do it."

"Whoa!" Lana stared at me with her mouth open and held her hands up, palms facing me. "One — I'm not the one who needs the life experience to write a song. Two — I didn't say it had to be that. I mean, you could go get a job at the diner, find yourself a sugar-daddy, take a road trip across America. Three — I've done it before."

"You have? What was it like? Who did it with you?"

I couldn't believe my roommate had swum naked. I tried to picture her with no clothes on, splashing someone in a river, moonlight bouncing off her bare shoulders, and I felt the heat rising in my cheeks.

"It was cool." She shrugged. "You should try it some time. It's liberating."

"Please, Lana. Please come with me. I promise I won't tell anyone, but I can't do this alone."

She narrowed her eyes at me, and then a smile spread across her face. "Okay, I'll come, but if we're doing this, we're doing this properly."

My stomach sank. "What do you mean?"

"I mean, if we're skinny-dipping, people need to know about it. What's the point of a secret experience? You want to live a little, Jade, and that's what we're going to do."

I told Aaron the next day when we had a free period. We were in the library. I had an essay to finish, and Aaron was reading a book about Elvis Presley.

He glanced up from the book and swallowed. "What? Why?"

"Lana said I need some life experience so that I can write song lyrics from the heart." I shrugged.

"So, you're going to write about skinny-dipping?"

The book was open to a picture of Elvis looking incredible in a purple shirt and black leather jacket, a guitar on his lap, playing to a small select audience. Elvis died way too young, but he'd seen plenty of the world during his lifetime. It suddenly made perfect sense to me that Lana was right: I knew nothing about anything, and I needed to live a little. I needed to shed the restraints of my Asian culture for good, and enjoy the life that was offered to me.

"No." I shook my head. "I'm going to write about how it feels to be naked in the water, to lie back in the water with the moonlight on my face, and know that's who I really am, the person underneath the handmade clothes."

Aaron scratched his neck. "Will you… won't you be nervous?"

"Of course, but there should be nothing wrong with taking our clothes off, Aaron. Don't you see? We need to write lyrics people want to hear, and all I know is what I've read in other people's books, and I'm pretty sure that would be plagiarism."

I could tell he wanted to argue the point, but eventually he said, "When are you doing this?"

"Tomorrow night. Are you in?"

"I don't know."

I felt guilty because even though I was sitting next to Aaron with Elvis Presley smiling at us from the pages of a hardbacked book, it was Sam I was thinking about.

The weather had cooled overnight. The sky was clear and solid blue the following morning, but there was a chill in the air, which raised goosebumps on my shoulders as I walked to my first class, and orange-brown leaves were starting to form loose carpets around the trees in the school yard.

"I hope Sam has some alcohol to bring tonight," Lana said as she headed in the opposite direction to her first class.

Sam was coming. When she'd said she'd mention it to the others, I'd secretly hoped she'd include Sam, but now that I recalled the girl I saw him with in the cafeteria and realized that even if he did come, and brought alcohol, she'd come along, too. I hoped they wouldn't get too excited in front of the rest of us. It was one thing for everyone to take their clothes off, but I wasn't ready to watch other people do more than that.

Aaron was quiet. It wasn't until we were waiting in line in the cafeteria, and he picked up a chicken salad and a can of soda, that he said, "Are you still going through with this?"

"Uh-huh." I couldn't look at him. "Are you coming?"

"Sure," he said. "Someone has to look out for you."

I didn't ask him what he meant. We were a group of kids swimming in the river; it wasn't like we were doing anything dangerous.

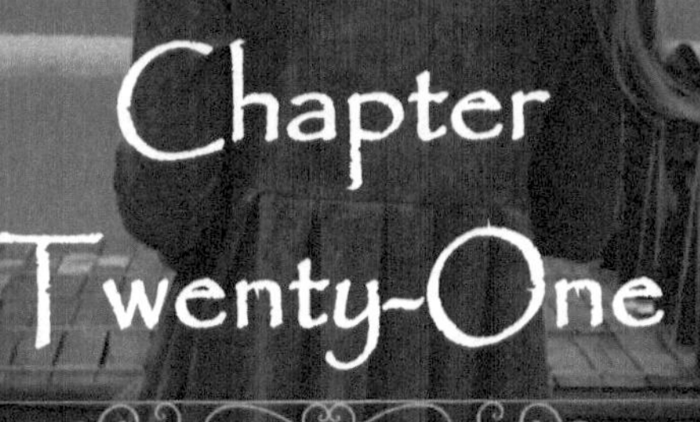

Chapter Twenty-One

Lana and I left our room, our towels rolled up under our arms, and met up with a couple of other girls Lana was friends with at the bottom of the stairs.

"Ready?" she asked.

They chatted as we left campus and headed away from town. I felt bad not waiting for Aaron, but he knew what time everyone was meeting, and he would probably tag along with Sam. It seemed strange to me, that in the period of a few weeks, I'd practically forgotten that Aaron and Sam were roommates, because when I looked at them, I saw how completely different they were, like planets circling the sun in opposite directions.

I shouldn't even have needed to worry because Sam and Aaron, and a load of other people, were already there when we arrived. Some were sprawled out on the riverbank. Others waited in small groups, discussing assignments and clubs and the football team try-outs.

Aaron came straight over to us, smiling, a navy and white striped towel slung over one shoulder. He rubbed his hands together, his shoulders hunched.

"The temperature has dropped," he said, glancing at the water, which looked almost black in the twilight, with silver ripples appearing and fading randomly.

"Ten out of ten for observation," said Lana. "It'll sort the pussies from the men."

The other girls roared with laughter, and they wandered off together, leaving me with Aaron. I was embarrassed that Lana had been rude, but part of me was worried that Aaron would try to hold me back;

something was telling me that this was going to be a pivotal moment in my life. It was almost as though my future hinged on doing this.

"What happens now?" he asked, peering around at the others. "Do we wait for someone to strip first?"

I shrugged. Nerves were kicking in. A quick glance around, and I hadn't yet spotted the blonde girl who Sam was seeing, and I wondered if she didn't want to come. Maybe she was more nervous that I was, and that strengthened my resolve to go through with it. I wondered what would happen once Aaron and I had seen each other with no clothes on.

Would it change things between us? Would I still be able to look him in the eye after, or would I constantly be reminded of this evening?

I didn't have the opportunity to voice my concerns out loud before squeals of laughter reached us from the group surrounding Sam, and I saw Lana dragging her sweater over her head. Aaron followed my gaze. I saw the way his shoulders tensed, and suddenly, I felt older, braver, more mature than I'd ever felt before. If I took my clothes off, I realized, he would have to do the same.

Without hesitating, and before I could talk myself out of it, I found a patch of dry grass to set my towel on and undid the zip of my jeans. A strange and excitable gurgle erupted from my throat. Aaron's towel landed on the grass beside mine, and he was pulling his sweater over his head, revealing his pale chest. As I slid my jeans down over my thighs, I felt a momentary panic that Aaron would notice the scars at the tops of my legs, but I shoved it aside – I wanted to bare my soul to the world, and that included my scars.

I kept my eyes focused on the water as I slipped my jeans down over my legs and dropped them onto the ground. I couldn't look at Aaron. Even when I felt his hand on mine, I flashed him a quick tentative smile, and then we were running, hand-in-hand, toward the river's edge.

The water hit with an icy jolt that took my breath away. I gasped as my head went underwater, my hair smothering my face, and rose to the surface spluttering. I pushed the hair out from my eyes and laughed out loud. Aaron laughed too, shaking water from his hair like a dog.

"Oh my god," I said. "This is brilliant."

Lana swam up behind me and leapt onto my shoulders, pushing me back under the water. I felt Aaron's grip on my upper arms as he lifted me back up.

"You did it!" yelled Lana above the sound of laughter and screams. "Welcome to the real world."

She swam off, and Aaron smoothed the hair away from my face. "Are you okay?"

I nodded. I didn't think I could speak; I was too emotional, caught up in the moment of knowing that the water was caressing my naked body. I was naked with a group of people I barely knew, and it felt amazing.

It wasn't long before our teeth were chattering. We swam to the riverbank and wrapped our towels around our shivering bodies, huddling together for warmth. Aaron radiated heat despite just having climbed out of the river with me, and I felt safe and comfortable with him.

"I'm glad you came," I said.

He wrapped an arm around my shoulders. "Your lips have turned blue, Jade," he murmured, hugging me close.

I peered into his eyes. I couldn't look away, and I felt his mouth moving toward mine, which seemed like the most natural thing in the world. Forgetting where we were, ignoring the way my legs shook with the chill, I leaned closer to him, my towel slipping from my shoulder.

Our lips were almost touching, Aaron's breath warming my face, when a hand grabbed mine, and I was lifted to my feet, barely clutching my towel around my chest.

Sam.

"Oh, no you don't," he said. "Dude, you can't keep Jade all to yourself. This is a party, man."

He was dragging me toward the others, where I saw Lana watching me while a girl was talking to her, and a boy I didn't recognize with his ass bared in my direction while he dried his legs with his towel. I glanced around at Aaron, who hadn't moved.

"Sorry," I whispered.

Sam made me sit beside him in the large circle that had formed beneath a big old tree. I leaned forward and gestured to Aaron to join us, but he was dragging his sweater over his head. When he was dressed, he came over, and I shifted closer to Sam so that Aaron could sit on the other side of me.

Maybe it was a conscious decision to keep Sam close to me, but it wasn't something I'd considered until I was squashed between them wearing only a towel. It gave me a quiver of excitement that I'd never experienced before, one that made me feel a little reckless.

I could tell that Aaron was tense beside me, his spine stiff, and I did nothing to make him relax. A bottle of something was being passed around. It reached Sam, and he took a large swig before handing it to me.

"What is it?" I asked.

"Drink," he said, tipping the bottle toward my mouth.

I took a sip and felt it warming me inside. I passed the bottle, smiling to Aaron, who also took a gulp before passing it on. My brain cells felt looser, the chill having melted away with the liquid in the bottle. I reached for Aaron's hand and squeezed it, and he smiled back at me, but then his eyes widened. I followed his gaze and saw Sam tipping some pills into the palm of his hand.

He must have sensed me watching because he swallowed one and offered mc his palm. I shook my head.

"Go on. Live a little, Jade."

My eyes sought out Lana, who was watching the scene pan out. I raised an eyebrow at her, and she shrugged as the bottle reached her again, and she tipped her head back.

"Jade?" Sam was staring at me.

"She said no," Aaron asserted, leaning across me and putting an arm out.

Sam didn't say anything but slipped the pills back into his pocket and turned his back on us.

The evening cooled for me after this, as though my skin suddenly recognized the chill in the air, my wet hair dripping down my back, my lack of clothes. Aaron seemed to notice that I wanted to leave, and he waited while I dressed, standing between me and the others who were growing rowdier with each sip of alcohol. I didn't glance at either Sam or Lana as we left; I didn't want to see their disappointment in me.

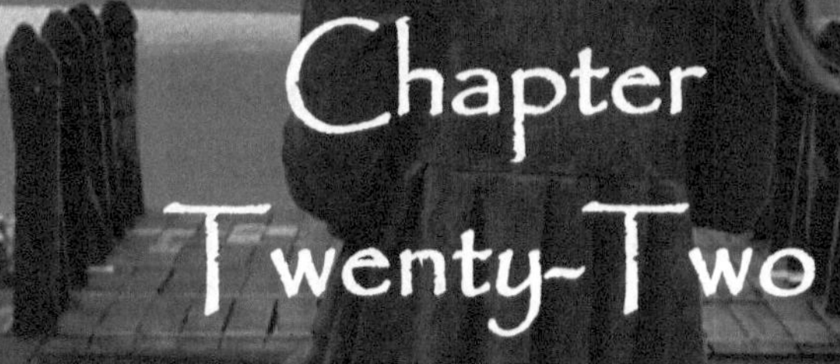

Chapter Twenty-Two

The following week, Sam was waiting outside the entrance to our dorm building when I returned after my classes. I kept my head down, although I'd spotted him as I crossed the courtyard and didn't make eye contact until I was standing beside him.

"Are you waiting for someone?" I asked.

"No, I saw a dinosaur in one of the windows, and I'm waiting for it to let me in." He grinned at me, his hair almost alive around his face. "Yes, I'm waiting for you. Come on." He took my arm, spun me around, and led me away from the school building.

"Where are we going?" I asked.

I peered over my shoulder to see if anyone else had spotted us leaving, but no one else was around.

"To the diner. I'm hungry."

"I've got an essay to finish." I stopped walking, but his grip on my arm was strong, and I found myself being propelled forward anyway.

"You can do that later, Jade. We need to eat first. Didn't anyone ever tell you that you can't write on a hungry brain?"

I laughed. "That's not a thing."

"Says who?"

"I don't know, but I've never heard it before."

"Just because you've never heard it, doesn't mean it isn't real."

We walked a few steps in silence.

"Is everyone else going to be there?" I asked.

"Where?"

"At the diner."

"Uh-huh."

I took a deep breath. "Will your girlfriend be there?"

He stopped abruptly, and I would have tripped over him had he not been gripping my arm so tightly. His eyebrows almost met in the middle. "My girlfriend?"

"The blonde girl. I saw you with her in the cafeteria, remember?"

He shook his head. "I have no idea who you're talking about, Jade, but I don't have a girlfriend."

"You don't?"

I didn't know why my heart raced with this news. It wasn't like Sam was interested in me; he could have had any girl he wanted, and he probably did.

We reached the parking lot behind the main building, and Sam beeped the lock on a beaten-up truck.

"Your carriage, milady."

He performed an elaborate bow and held the door open for me, closing it behind me after I was safely inside.

It felt weird sitting in such close proximity to Sam while he drove. I wondered if Lana had been in his truck the night he brought her home drunk. My stomach twisted, and my cheeks grew hot, when I thought about them kissing. Had Lana slept with

Sam? Would she tell me if she had? It wasn't like we were best friends or anything.

And then there was Aaron. Things had been a little awkward between us since the night we all went skinny-dipping, quiet; neither of us had mentioned the almost-kiss, but it sat there between us like a sack of wheat. Maybe Aaron would be at the diner. A thought struck me then, that maybe Aaron had spoken to Sam about this, and he was trying to set us up together.

But there was no one at the diner when we arrived. It was still early, and the others might have still been in class.

"When are the others getting here?" I asked.

"Later," said Sam. The waitress came and took our orders, and he sat back watching me. "So, what's with you and Aaron?"

"What do you mean?"

He leaned forward slowly, his eyes fixated on mine. "You know what I mean. Are you two a couple or what?"

"No." I shook my head. "We're friends. We went to high school together. We want to start a band."

Sam gave a low whistle. "A band, huh? Can you sing?"

"Yes. Everyone says I'm good."

"Go on then — sing something for me."

He sat back again, arms folded across his chest.

My face felt hot, and I glanced around at the few customers who were in the diner, enjoying their burgers and fries.

"Not in here," I said.

"Why not? Are you scared I won't think you're good?"

"No."

"Why not, then? Go on, Jade, I dare you."

I swallowed, trying to think of a good reason not to sing in front of Sam. I didn't think the other customers would mind; it wasn't like I was going to stand up and belt out a whole Tina Turner song. Was it because I couldn't bear for him to not think I was good enough?

I took a deep breath and sang a few lines from one of the songs I'd learned from *West Side Story*. The other customers stared at me from above their food; a couple smiled, one shook his head and took a bite of his hot dog.

When I was finished, Sam was grinning at me. "Wow, Jade Xiu, that was actually good."

"So, you thought I was joking?"

He shrugged. "Not really, you just don't strike me as someone who's confident enough to stand up and sing in front of people."

I laughed. "I was sitting down."

"So, what then, you want to be a singer some day?"

"Yes. Aaron is good, too. We performed together at summer camp."

Our food arrived, and Sam waited until the waitress had walked away before he spoke.

"How many Asian singers do you know?"

I stared at my fries. It was true — I couldn't think of any. But anyone could sing. I mean, it was like being an athlete, or a gymnast, or an actress; you were talented at one thing or another, and race or culture didn't have any influence over what someone could or couldn't do. A lot of Americans couldn't sing. Some of them were probably great footballers or scientists, and a lot of Asian Americans were probably great singers.

My mind was racing around what he had said, attempting to work it out in my own head, because I didn't understand if he was being mean or not.

Eventually I said, "Just because you haven't heard of any, doesn't mean they don't exist."

Sam's smile grew even wider. "I like you, Jade," he said.

After that, Sam was often hanging around me after class, waiting to take me to the diner, or to go for a walk around the valley. Sometimes, when it was extra cold, we sat in the library together away from the doors so that no one would spot us together. I hadn't said anything to Aaron, and I didn't want any rumors getting back to him. If anything happened between Sam and I, I wanted to tell him myself.

Sam's family was quite wealthy. He said that his mom was a model when she was younger, and his dad owned a nationwide chain of boutiques. They had a massive house in Philly, and a villa in Florida, and regularly took vacations to Mexico or Bermuda or Hawaii.

He didn't ask about my family, and I didn't offer him any information. I hadn't written to my mother since I arrived, and I knew that I should, but I couldn't quite match up my life here to my life at home, and so it was easier to keep them separate.

I was spending less and less time with Aaron too, and I knew that he thought it was because of what happened on the riverbank, but I didn't know how to explain that I was attracted to Sam in a way that I wasn't to Aaron.

The other thing that worried me, and this was what occupied most of my thoughts whenever I was alone and not working on an assignment, was the similarity between Sam and Logan. They both came from families who had money. They were both handsome and knew it. And I'd seen them both with other girls who looked nothing like me.

I kept telling myself that Sam wasn't Logan, that he had no reason to play the same game, that he was friends with, and in all probability had kissed, Lana, and she was Asian American, too. But still, I kept the barriers up, kept him at arms' length, and I didn't even kiss him until Lana told me one evening that Sam had told her how much he liked me.

"Really? He said that?" I struggled to keep the excitement from my voice.

"Uh-huh." She was reading a Jacqueline Susann novel.

"What do you think I should do?" I sat on the end of her bed.

She placed the book face down on her lap and stared at me. "I'm not your pesky aunt, Jade. I don't give relationship advice."

I chewed my bottom lip. I'd still not even begun to write a song for the band Aaron's friend was starting up, and if anything, I'd felt even more confused since the whole skinny-dipping experience. Maybe Lana was right — I had nothing to give to a song that people would remember. It was time to pull down the barriers and start living my life, even if that meant I might get hurt along the way.

Chapter Twenty-Three

Over the next few weeks, the amount of time I spent with Sam kind of crept up on me, until it seemed like not a day had gone by when we didn't see each other. I was busy with drama club, and A Capella, and science assignments which I had even less interest in now that I was at college.

Each time I thought I'd had an idea for a song, I wrote a couple of lines and then realized how dull and childish they sounded. I needed to speak to Aaron about my feelings for him, which seemed to have faded in comparison to my feelings for Sam, but I was worried because if he reacted badly, our friendship might suffer, and it would all be my fault. I was still struggling to make friends with other girls, and I knew that if I wasn't sharing a room with Lana, our relationship would be non-existent.

All these concerns were making me feel exhausted because, while I could switch off during lessons and lectures, at night, they all bounced around inside my brain until I thought my head might explode.

Then one morning, Aaron was waiting for me outside the dorm building, a wide grin on his face. I quickly glanced around to check that Sam wasn't coming to meet me, before asking him what had happened.

"Gabe wants us to audition for the band!" His eyes were bright, his smile so huge I could see his back teeth; he was so excited, he could barely stand still.

"What? When?"

"Tonight! He wants to hear us sing together. He said he wasn't sure about having a female lead, but he heard you at A Capella and says your tone is exactly what he was looking for."

"He—he heard me?"

I was trying to process everything Aaron was saying, and my brain felt like it was brimful of information. We were going to audition for a band. Alright, it was only a small band put together by a kid at college, but everyone had to start somewhere, and we were going to audition tonight. Together. And we still didn't have a song.

"I haven't finished writing the song yet," I said. That was an understatement.

"It doesn't matter, Jade." Aaron shook his head. "Choose a song, something loud, rocky, something we both know, because I haven't told you the best bit."

"There's more?"

"He's arranged a small gig in town next month."

"We're playing a gig?"

"Well, if he likes us, we are. Which, of course, he will, because what's not to like? He'll love you, Jade; I know he will." He reached for my hand and squeezed it. "This is what you've been waiting for."

He was right. This was what I'd been waiting for since I was old enough to change the radio stations on my parents' radio from the Chinese stations they listened to, to one that played the Rolling Stones, Sonny and Cher, and Fleetwood Mac. I had a brief vision of myself as the next Stevie Nicks, and my eyes brimmed with tears because it dawned on me that Aaron's excitement was aimed solely at me. He wasn't doing this for himself; he was doing this for me.

I threw my arms around his neck and hugged him, breathing in the smell of his shampoo. I released him and stood back.

"What shall we sing? Can we practice during lunch? Where is the audition? What should I wear?"

Aaron laughed loudly and took my hand as we walked to class. There was no way I was going to be able to concentrate knowing we had an audition that evening.

"You choose a song. Yes. In a barn outside of town — it's owned by a family friend. Something sexy."

The last sentence stopped me in my tracks. It wasn't so much because I didn't own anything sexy, but more because it was the sort of comment I would expect to hear from Sam, not Aaron.

Aaron's smile faded. "Sorry," he said. "I don't know why I said that. You always look amazing in whatever you're wearing. I think I was just… well… I was thinking Stevie Nicks." He shrugged.

"That's okay," I said. "So was I."

I was supposed to go to the park with Sam later; he was playing football first, and then we were going to head to the diner. I would have to catch him before lunch to let him know that I couldn't make it because I was going for an audition. I was so excited, even my thoughts were squealing inside my brain.

"Suit yourself," said Sam.

I found him in the hallway between classes, and now he turned and walked away, head down.

"Wait! What's wrong?" I called out to his back.

He turned around to face me but continued walking backwards. "Nothing's wrong, Jade. You go along to your audition. It's what you want, right?"

I nodded. It *was* what I wanted; he knew it was, but I couldn't understand why he was being so off about it.

"I'll see you around then." And he was gone.

I didn't tell Aaron about Sam's reaction; he still didn't know that I'd been spending more time with his roommate, and I was convinced Sam hadn't said anything because I was certain Aaron would have told me.

I was confused and a little unsettled by it, but I pushed it to the back of my mind so that I could focus on the audition. I would think about Sam after. I'd done nothing wrong and was probably imagining that there was something wrong when really, he would see me tomorrow and be excited to hear all about it.

We were going to sing *Don't Stop Believing*. It was a song we both loved, and was one that we could sing together, our voices complementing each other. We practiced in the music room at lunch. After classes, Lana was in the room when I went back to get changed. She was impressed when I told her and loaned me a pair of green ripped jeans, with sequins sewn onto the pockets, and a black lace blouse to wear. She even helped me do my makeup, coating my eyelids in sparkly green eye shadow with a flick of black liner in each corner. I barely recognized myself when I looked in the mirror.

"Now you're ready," she said. "If you don't look the part, you won't sound the part." She gave me a hug, and it brought fresh tears to my eyes.

The band was already set up when we arrived at the barn. It wasn't as big as I'd expected, although

I'd never been inside a barn before. There were huge bundles of hay stacked on one side, but Gabe had the drums and guitars positioned in the center of the building, two mics set up in front, with huge speakers on either side of the barn.

I was so nervous, my mouth felt dry, and my throat clicked when I tried to speak. Aaron had brought a bottle of water, and he told me not to panic; I was going to be amazing. We had a little trouble with the mics at first, but once Gabe got them sorted and we started, I forgot about everything apart from the lyrics we were singing, and the sounds of our voices together.

When we finished, the musicians clapped, and Gabe came straight over to tell us that he loved our sound, and he wanted us to play the gig at a small party next month. I wanted to jump up and down with excitement, but instead, I nodded and said, "Yes, please."

"We want to trial a new tune, though," said Gabe. "How soon can you get your song finished?"

I swallowed.

"How soon do you need it?" asked Aaron.

"Like yesterday."

It was three days before I saw Sam crossing the playing field with one of his friends. I wanted to ask Aaron if Sam had been acting strange lately, but I was too scared to in case Aaron realized there was something going on. I couldn't tell him now. Not yet. Not until we'd finished writing the song and played the first gig. I promised myself that I would tell him after the gig.

"Hello, stranger," Sam said when he saw me. He flashed me his beautiful smile, and I couldn't help but smile back. "Where have you been hiding?"

"Nowhere," I said. I wanted to say that it felt like Sam was the one hiding, but I didn't. "I've been busy. I'm writing a song with Aaron."

"Yeah, he mentioned that." Sam glanced around as if checking to make sure no one was listening, but he didn't ask about the audition or the gig. "Coming out later? I've missed you."

I chewed my bottom lip. I was supposed to be meeting Aaron at the library — the song was almost finished, although we didn't know yet if it was any good. "I can't, sorry."

Sam shrugged and turned to walk away. "That's twice you've knocked me back, Jade. I won't wait around forever."

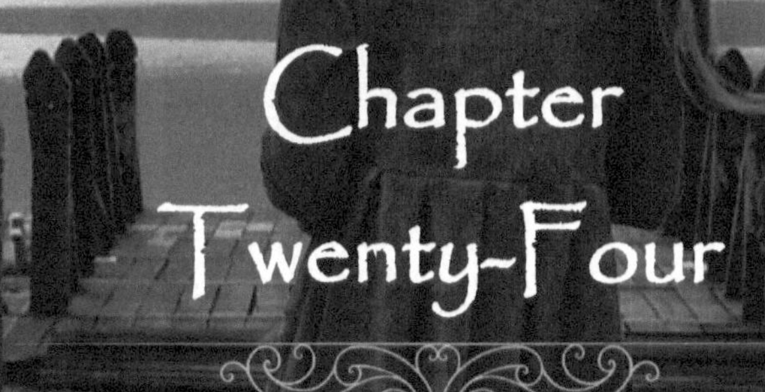

Chapter Twenty-Four

Aaron and I rehearsed every evening with the band. Gabe liked our song, but it was a work in progress that kept evolving for a few days after we performed it for the first time. We changed lyrics, added some, and then deleted them again, the music adapting to them each time we sang. We were going to be playing for forty-five minutes, which was a lot of time to fill, and Gabe kept reminding us that we were not only singing to an audience, but we were also performing to them, getting them to believe in our lyrics the way we believed in them.

I'd taken Sam's comment to heart, and so every evening after we left the barn, tired and buzzed with adrenaline, I waited until Aaron had headed back to the boys' dorms before I snuck back out to meet Sam. He said that he was happy to wait for me if it meant that he got my full attention, which was as exhausting as singing the same songs on repeat. I clung to every word he said, smiled whenever he looked at me, and laughed at his jokes.

When his friends tagged along, I hung back until Sam came over and slipped an arm around my shoulder and kissed the top of my head the way he'd kissed the blonde girl in the cafeteria.

It was all worth it, I told myself, for that simple intimate gesture of affection.

One Saturday evening, a few weeks after the audition, we rehearsed until late. My throat felt sore, and I was shaky because I hadn't eaten for hours, but someone Sam knew was having a party just outside of town, and he wanted me to go.

I rushed back to my room to change, telling Aaron that I was behind on an assignment, and Lana had offered to help. I felt guilty when he smiled and said that he would read it through for me when I was finished, but I was too tired to dwell on it. After the gig, I told myself I would come clean, and then I wouldn't have to keep lying to my best friend.

Lana was doing her makeup when I reached the room. "You're late," she said.

"Are you going to the party?" I asked.

She was wearing a short black dress and Doc Martens, and she looked stunning. I'd planned on wearing a black dress too, but now I realized that I didn't have anything else to wear, and we would look ridiculous turning up in identical clothes.

"Where else did you think I was going?" She looked down at her clothes.

I would have to go in the clothes I was wearing. "Are you getting a ride with Sam?"

"Sam left earlier. You can come with me if you like?"

My stomach sank. He'd gone without me. I hoped he wouldn't be in a mood with me; I'd told him we were rehearsing, and he'd offered to wait. It wasn't like I just didn't show.

"Sure, thanks," I said,

Sam was already drunk when we arrived. Lana left me as soon as we went inside. "Don't think I'm playing gooseberry," she said.

"Jade." Sam leaned heavily on my shoulders, held his glass to my lips, and tipped it up for me to drink.

I swallowed and grimaced as the liquid burned my insides.

He laughed and patted my head like I was a dog. "Here, have some more."

I shook my head. "I can't," I said. "I'm rehearsing all day tomorrow. The gig's next week."

I waited for him to smile, to tell me he was proud of me, to acknowledge how important this was to me, but instead, his mouth twisted into a tight bud.

"I'm starting to think you don't like me anymore."

"Don't be silly," I said. "You know how important this is to me; I told you when I first met you that I wanted to sing. I'm just tired."

He wiggled a finger in front of my face. "You're always tired. Too tired for me these days, Jade Xiu. I'll have to find someone else to dance with." He stared at me, daring me to let him find another dance partner, one who wasn't tired.

I took the plastic cup from his hand and took a large gulp. I wished I'd eaten because my head already felt fuzzy, but I wanted to have fun with Sam. I didn't want him to dance with anyone else; I wanted him to be with me.

So, when he offered me a pill later in the evening, when the room was already spinning around me, and told me that it would stop me from feeling tired, give me a buzz, I swallowed it.

He didn't warn me how exhaustion would creep up on me like a slow-filling bath when the buzz wore off. In the ensuing days, he gave me a pill when I was quiet, a pill when I had no appetite, and another pill when the puffy circles under my eyes looked like bruises. He insisted on seeing me every night after rehearsals, which meant that I had to make more excuses to Aaron and find my way around town without a ride.

Then he announced that his folks wanted to take him to dinner at a restaurant in Philly, and they wanted to meet me. It was the first time he had mentioned introducing me to his family, and my heart leapt around inside my chest as though I'd just run a full lap around the athletic track.

"You told them about me?" I asked.

I could hardly believe it — I was going to meet his family. I'd felt a sharp stab of pain when I no longer got to spend time with Jen's family, as for a while when we were younger, I'd almost come to think of them as mine, but it didn't matter now. I imagined that Sam's family would be like Jen's, welcoming, warm, their home bright and sunny, and filled with the aroma of freshly-baked cookies.

"Saturday…," he was still speaking.

"What? This Saturday?"

"Yeah, why, what's the problem?" He was no longer smiling, and his eyes had turned hard and dark.

"The gig is on Saturday," I said.

How could he have forgotten? I'd spoken about nothing else since the audition… and then I realized that Sam never wanted to speak about my singing, or the band, or the gig, and changed the subject whenever I mentioned it.

He gave me a tight-lipped smile and shrugged. "Take it or leave it, Jade. Up to you."

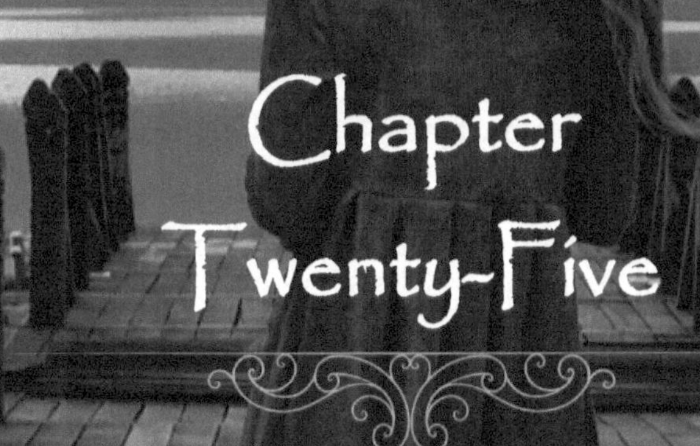

Chapter Twenty-Five

The next rehearsal didn't go well. I could barely string two words together in tune, and at one point, I sank to the floor in tears.

Aaron knelt beside me, an arm around my shoulders. "What's wrong, Jade?" His eyes looked worried, and there were frown lines across his forehead. "Are you sick? You haven't seemed right the last few days."

I shook my head and brushed the tears away.

"I'm tired," I said in a scrawny voice.

I was such a coward. I couldn't tell Aaron about Sam, and I couldn't tell Sam that the gig was the most important thing in the world to me, even more important than meeting his parents. I was so emotionally drained, so confused and excited and scared about everything that was going on in my life, that I didn't think to question why I couldn't be honest with either of them — and there was no one I could speak to about it.

I thought about Jen. If she were in the same situation, she would speak to her mom about it, and I knew what her mom would say, that she'd already made up her mind when she said that the gig was the most important thing in the world.

But it wasn't that simple. I saw being in a potential relationship with Sam in the same way I saw people looking at me as an all-American girl. I hoped it would be like donning a cloak that would suddenly make my Asian legacy disappear. I began to question whether I would ever make it as a rock star. There were no guarantees — plenty of people could sing, and they weren't all famous.

Without even realizing I was doing it, I gradually talked myself out of showing up for the gig: there would be other opportunities, I told myself; this was only one small spot playing to no more than a hundred people, no big deal. If I was good enough to make it, someone would recognize it, and I'd be catapulted into stardom like so many other young stars. I talked myself around in circles until my brain was spinning like a top, second-guessing what Sam and Aaron would say, and contradicting myself.

On the day of the gig, I waited for Sam outside the boys' dorm, praying that Aaron would not come outside first. Mid-morning, when my legs were numb from standing around, and my stomach was growling with hunger, Sam approached me from the direction of town, with another boy I only vaguely recognized because he was a couple of years older than us.

He didn't spot me until we were almost close enough to touch. His eyes were bloodshot, and his skin pale.

"Have you been out all night?" I asked.

"Jade?" He narrowed his eyes at me as if I were standing with the sunlight behind me when the day was overcast and cloudy. "What are you doing here?"

"I—I want to speak to you. It's about tonight."

He shook his head. "What about tonight?"

"I—I can't come to Philly with you. I can't let the band down."

He turned his face and stared out across the courtyard. Then he shrugged. "It's your life, Jade."

He went to walk inside, the other boy following him. Sam stopped with the door half-open and glanced at me over his shoulder.

"You should've said you didn't want to be my girlfriend. I could've found someone else to take with me." He went inside, the door slamming behind him.

I crossed the courtyard, my brain as numb as my feet, which were tingling now that I was moving about. I didn't know what to think. Why had he not said he wanted me to be his girlfriend? I'd have tried to be more like how a girlfriend was supposed to be, if he had spoken the words out loud. I'd have gone to the diner with him. I'd have watched his football matches. I'd have spent less time with Aaron.

Lana was still asleep when I let myself back into our room. I flopped onto my bed, and she opened an eye and looked at me. "Where have you been?"

"Waiting for Sam. He said he wanted me to be his girlfriend." I stared at the ceiling, at a spider that was making its webby home in the corner above the door.

Lana shook her head and propped it on one elbow. "He said that? Wow! I had no idea you guys were so serious, I mean…"

"Neither did I. He wants me to have dinner with his parents tonight."

She stared at me then. "You're singing tonight though, right?"

"I don't know what to do." I rolled onto my side so that I was facing her.

"Why are we even having this conversation? If you want to be a singer, you go sing."

"But… Sam said he'll take someone else if I don't want to be his girlfriend."

"And?"

"And I do want to be his girlfriend."

Lana slid her legs over the side of the bed and sat up. "Listen, Jade, Sam's a great guy, and yeah, he's cute, and I can see why girls throw themselves at him. But if he told me that he was taking someone else, I would let him. The guy can be a dick when he wants to be, and you're better than that."

Her words stung, and I blinked back tears. She was only jealous because he wasn't interested in her when she had the chance. But it was her last words that hit like a cup of cold water. *You're better than that.* Because when I thought about it, really thought about everything that I was, my family, my culture, even my grades, I knew that I wasn't better than that.

I told Aaron I was pulling out of the band.

"You're what?" He stared at me, open-mouthed. "Why?"

I turned around and walked back to the dorm. I didn't want to look at him because I could see the shock in his eyes, and I didn't want to wait for the disappointment to follow.

"Jade, wait!" He fell into step beside me, but I didn't slow down. "Tell me why? What happened? The rehearsals have been going so well. The guys are really excited about tonight. I'm excited. I thought you were, too."

I ignored him. When I reached the dorm, I didn't even glance at Aaron, expecting him to turn around and walk away, so that I could go to my room and cry into my pillow. I didn't know if I was doing the right thing, but I couldn't shake the feeling that I was never going to be good enough to be a singer, and that this was the only route left for me to finally escape my culture. I had to be with an American boy and be accepted into his American family.

But Aaron followed me inside.

As the door slammed, I finally looked at him. "What are you doing? You're not allowed in here."

"I don't care," said Aaron. "I'm not letting you do this. I know how important this is to you, and I'm not going to stand back and let you throw it away."

I walked up the stairs, Aaron one step behind me. Along the hallway, and he was still there keeping up with me.

Lana glanced up from her book when we walked in together. She shook her head and returned to the page in front of her.

"Tell me why," Aaron said. "What's changed? I thought you wanted this."

"I do," I said, slipping my sneakers off. I wanted him to leave so that I could curl up in my bed with the duvet over my head and wake up tomorrow when it would all be over. "I did. I don't want to talk about it."

Aaron grabbed my elbow and spun me around to face him. "Is this about Sam? Because if it is…" He shook his head. "You can't trust him, Jade. Please listen to me. I've seen the way he is around girls, and I don't trust him."

"But I do!" I snapped.

Aaron dropped my arm and stared at me. And there it was… the disappointment I'd been dreading. "Please don't do this, Jade. You have to sing tonight. The band won't be the same without you, and this is what you want to do. This is only the start of it. Please don't bail before you've even begun."

Tears trickled down my cheeks. "I'm sorry," I mumbled, my throat thick with all the tears waiting to come.

"Lana!" Aaron said. "Tell her, please. Tell her not to be so stupid."

Lana looked at us and shrugged. "I'm not her mother."

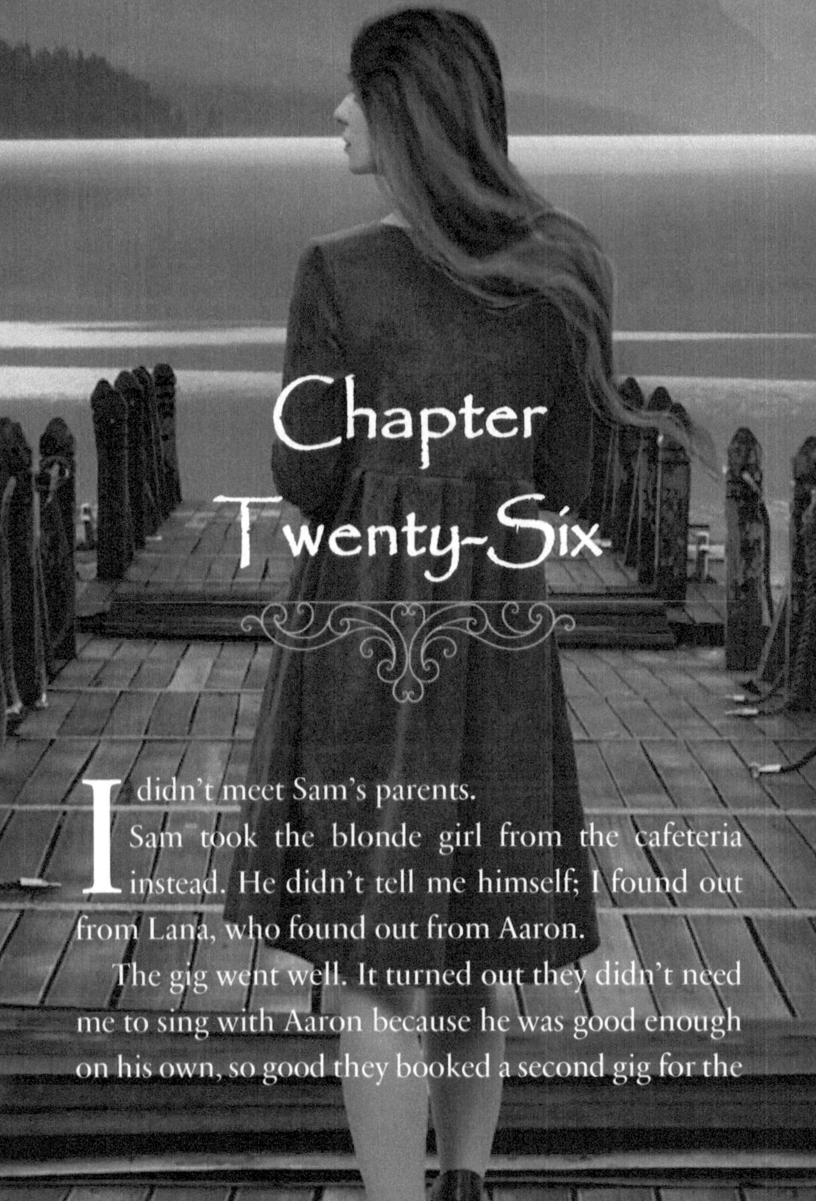

Chapter Twenty-Six

I didn't meet Sam's parents.

Sam took the blonde girl from the cafeteria instead. He didn't tell me himself; I found out from Lana, who found out from Aaron.

The gig went well. It turned out they didn't need me to sing with Aaron because he was good enough on his own, so good they booked a second gig for the following month, this one a bit larger in a youth club in town. I found this out from Lana, too.

I stopped going to class. The pupil liaison officer sent me a note asking me to go to her office because she was concerned about my grades dropping and my lack of attendance, but I didn't keep the appointment.

I had no energy. I'd never been so lethargic in my life before, and I put it down to hunger — I couldn't remember the last meal I ate. Lana would bring me food several times a day, set it on the floor by my bed, and then take it away again the following day when it was cold and stale and crusty. I had no appetite because I had no energy.

My thoughts drifted to my mother, who had always been buzzing with life, always working, running errands, doing chores around the house or cooking. She only sat still late at night and even then, she would be practicing her English words or running cloth through the sewing machine to make clothes for us all.

Lana would sit on the edge of my bed in the evenings after classes, brush my hair, stroke my cheek, and ask me to eat something, to talk to her about it because everything felt better after you got it off your chest.

"Jade, why don't you come outside for a little while?" she asked one afternoon. "It's warm today. It'll do you good; you have no color in your cheeks."

I rolled over and stared at the wall until she went away.

The following evening, she snuck Aaron into the room. I pretended to be asleep. I heard the hiss of their whispers, sensed the shrugs and the way they rolled their eyes at each other. Eventually, the door opened and closed again, and I waited a few minutes before I rolled over and found Aaron standing there watching me.

He smiled when I looked at him. I didn't have the energy to smile back, and my lips were too dry and cracked and scabbed from where I'd picked them during the long dull hours when Lana was out of the room.

"Jade." He stroked the hair away from my face and held a glass of water to my lips, raising my head so that it wouldn't spill over the pillow. I swallowed, and my throat felt sore and tight. "Will you please eat something? How about I bring you some soup? It'll make you feel better."

I wanted to tell him that I didn't want to feel better, that nothing would make me feel better because I'd let everyone down, including myself.

Mostly myself. Hot tears squeezed from my eyes, and I said, "I'm not hungry," surprised at how croaky my voice sounded.

"You haven't eaten in… in days," he said. "You'll get sick if you don't eat."

He sounded like my mother, so I closed my eyes.

"I need you to get well, Jade, so that you can come back to the band. They… we want you to sing with us at the next gig."

I opened my eyes and looked at him through my tears, his kind face blurring and floating around in front of me. They still wanted me to sing with them. Maybe I hadn't ruined everything.

I closed my eyes, and when I opened them again, Aaron was gone, and it was dark. I could tell that Lana wasn't in her bed because the cover was flat. My thoughts, numbed by enforced hunger and apathy, suddenly flooded back with a vengeance, making my brain thump inside my skull and my knees shake. I wasn't sure if I'd been dreaming, but I thought I recalled Aaron telling me that the band still wanted me to sing with them. I didn't understand why they would still want me after I had let them down so badly.

I tried to sit up and had to press my forehead against the cool wall to stop myself from being sick;

my body was trembling all over, and waves of hot sickness and icy shivers washed over me.

I knew what I had to do.

I needed to sort my thoughts into some kind of order so that I could forget about Sam and focus on my dreams again, and there was only one way I knew how to do that. Pushing the covers aside, I dragged my legs over the side of the bed and tried to stand. It took three attempts before I could stay upright, although the room spun around me, and I had to swallow back bile and squeeze my eyes closed to stop myself from vomiting over the floor.

Lana had left the light switched off when she went out, probably because I was sleeping, and when I reached my desk, I ran my hands across the surface, knocking over the jar of pens before I found my pencil case. Slumping onto my knees, I tugged at the zip of the case and rummaged inside until my fingers located the compass. The sharp point pricked my finger, and I gasped, leaning back against the bed. It was enough to bring my thoughts back into focus.

Raising my top to reveal my bare tummy, I pushed my pajama bottom down, but didn't have the energy to raise my butt off the floor and slide them down over my thighs, so I sat back and pushed the point into the soft flesh above my hips.

Then everything went black.

Chapter Twenty-Seven

Aaron came to visit me in the hospital. He brought candy and sunny yellow flowers to brighten the place up, and told me how much he missed me around campus.

"Gabe and the guys send their best wishes," he said. "They're still waiting for you to come back."

I looked at him without speaking; there were plenty of words in my head, but none of them seemed to make sense anymore. They were jumbled up like dirty laundry. That was how I felt, like dirty laundry. Some were discarded, waiting to be cleaned and reused, and cast aside again. Tears squeezed from the corners of my eyes, and Aaron reached for my cold hand and held it between his to make it warm again.

He didn't look at the bandage around my wrist. It was like a white ghost lurking in the corner of the room that we hoped might go away if we didn't acknowledge its presence.

I didn't recall setting out to seriously harm myself. The point of the compass must have slipped, I don't know, or maybe I landed on it when I lost consciousness, but now the doctors questioned me every day about my state of mind and what had prompted me to do such a thing. I felt like a butterfly trying to sneak back into its cocoon because it was frightened of the big scary world.

"Sorry, Jade," Aaron said when he saw the tears. "No pressure. I didn't realize I was putting so much pressure on you. You need to take some time out for yourself, from the band, from school, from everything, get yourself well again."

He was rambling, but I wasn't paying attention. He thought I should drop out of school. I wondered if that was what everyone thought, that I couldn't cope with being away from home and at college, and I was filled with panic that my parents would think that too, and they would come take me back, where I'd be trapped in their blanketed Chinese world forever.

My heartrate was speeding up, and my breathing ragged, whistling through my sore throat. I shook my head at Aaron and snatched my hand away from him.

"I'm—I'm fine," I managed. "I—I need to—to get up."

I tried sitting forward, but I was attached to a drip by a long snaking tube, which tugged against the stand by the side of the bed. It rattled, and Aaron had to stop it from tipping sideways and onto the floor.

"Stay where you are, Jade," he said. "I'll get someone to help." He pressed a shiny red button on the wall above the bed, and a nurse appeared a few moments later, in her white uniform and her flat efficient shoes.

"Everything okay, Jade?" she asked, reaching for my unbandaged wrist to check my pulse. "Have we had a little too much excitement for one day?"

Aaron's gaze flickered between me and the nurse, his eyes filled with concern.

"She was trying to sit up," he said.

"Here," said the nurse, setting my arm gently down on the bed, "let me help." She leaned across me and hoisted me up the bed, plumping the pillows behind me for support. "Better?"

I nodded. I couldn't look at her. I didn't want to sit up. I didn't want to be here. I no longer had any idea where I wanted to be.

"Here's the magazine your friend brought for you. How about I leave it on the side of the bed here so that you can reach it?"

Lana had visited the day before and brought a copy of my favorite magazine and a bottle of soda because she said I looked like I needed to fizz up a bit.

"Gave me a scare," she said. "I wish you'd told me how bad you were feeling. I'd have punched Sam in the nose and stopped him from looking so pretty."

Her words had wrung more tears from me. I hadn't thought about how my actions might affect Lana, and I'd been so used to wandering through life alone, that I'd left it too late to realize that I had found a friend who was looking out for me in her own way.

Now, I closed my eyes and waited for Aaron and the nurse to leave me alone.

I slept, and when I awoke, my parents were sitting in plastic chairs by the side of my bed, looking small and old and uncomfortable. I blinked as though I might make them disappear.

My mother sat forward when she realized I was awake and reached for my hand.

"Jade," she said in her strong accent, "you are awake."

"Ma," I said, tears streaming down my cheeks. "You're—you're here."

I could smell the lemon scent of her clothes, which made me think of home. I saw the silvery-gray streaks that had appeared in her hair since I left home, saw the lines fanning out from the corners of her eyes. She was still petite, still wiry, still so bundled up with fidgety energy that it tired me just watching her.

I glanced at my father, who had been reading a newspaper. He folded it across his lap now and smiled at me.

"Yù," he said. "You're okay?"

I nodded. How could I tell them that I had never felt less okay in my life? I had wanted to be a typical American teenager, going to college and doing what other teenagers did, but I'd also tried to be a good Chinese American daughter, obedient, intelligent, and dedicated to carving out a decent future for myself. And I had failed at both. I'd let everyone down.

An attendant came into the room with my foil-wrapped dinner on a plastic tray, which she slid onto the mobile rest and pushed across the bed. The smell of meat and gravy made me feel nauseous, and I tried to push it away.

Instantly, my mother was on her feet and moving it away from me. "I bring you Chinese noodle soup," she said.

I shook my head. "I'm not hungry, Ma."

But she wasn't listening. She reached into the large bag on the floor beside her and brought out a Thermos with a plastic cup placed over the screw-top lid. Into the cup, my mother poured steaming chicken noodle soup. It smelled like the kitchen at home, where I had helped her prepare and cook so many meals over the years, that I almost believed I was back there. Joseph was already seated and waiting for his food, and Ma had her back to me, slicing vegetables while I stirred.

She raised the cup to my lips and waited for me to drink. "It make you feel better," she said. "Give you strength."

And she was right. The first sip scalded my tongue, but as I swallowed, I felt the warmth traveling through me and lighting me up from the inside out. I almost finished the cup and leaned back against the pillows, my cheeks flushed. I realized that I felt more alive than I had been in weeks.

My mother touched the bandage around my wrist, tears welling in her eyes. "We did wrong thing, Jade, coming to America. This not happen in China."

I felt lightheaded suddenly, my thoughts buzzing around inside my skull. I didn't want them to think that. I didn't want them to take me back to China; I would not be able to bear it, returning to a life that was so restricted and so regimented.

"What? No," I said. "It has nothing to do with that."

"Why then?" she asked. "Why you do this to yourself? Why you not happy?"

I opened my mouth to protest that I *was* happy, but the words would not come. When I thought about it, I couldn't remember if I had ever been truly happy. It felt as though I had spent my entire life pulling in the opposite direction of my parents, constantly battling to escape the culture I was born into, that now, sitting in this hospital room with machines beeping around me, I felt as though I had been looking the wrong way while my childhood passed me by.

Tears trickled down my cheeks and pooled onto my pajama top, and I did nothing to stop them. My mother put her arms around my shoulders, and I sobbed against her, clinging to the feel of her bony arms and the lemon-haze around her. Little Yù was gone, and I would never get her back.

When the sobs died down, my mother released me. "We take you home for a while, Jade. You rest. You get strong. We—"

"No." I shook my head vigorously and had to cling to the cover while my brain cells settled. "No, I don't want to come home. I'll be fine. I—I won't do it again. I—"

The nurse came in to take my temperature. She had kind gray eyes and a wide smile, her top teeth a little crooked.

"Did I hear your mom say that she wants to take you home, Jade?" she asked, one hand on my wrist and the other checking her pocket-watch. I opened my mouth, and she slipped a thermometer under my tongue. "I think that's a great idea. It will do you a world of good. It's unlikely the doctor will sign your release papers and send you straight back to college."

I shook my head, feeling like a bird with a broken wing. I didn't want to go back home. I couldn't. My life was here now. Aaron was here, and Lana, and what about my studies? With the prospect of not graduating from college hanging in front of me, I realized how important my education was to me. It felt as though my entire future was balancing on the summit of a mountain – one push, and I'd go hurtling down the other side and disappear, never to be seen again.

The nurse must have seen the fear in my eyes. "Stop panicking, Jade. Your body has been through a trauma, and it is going to take time to heal. You must start looking after yourself, and if that means taking a break from education," she shrugged, "then it isn't the end of the world. You can pick up again next semester, or next year. Lots of people do it and go on to have highly successful careers. Don't beat yourself up over it." She scribbled some notes on the chart at the end of my bed and smiled at my parents. "You take good care of her. Some TLC is exactly what she needs right now."

I wanted to scream at her that my parents didn't know what TLC meant, that TLC wasn't something that existed in Chinese families, but I didn't. I no longer had the energy to fight back.

Chapter Twenty-Eight

It had only been a few months since I left home to go to college, and yet I felt like a little girl when I returned home. It felt like only yesterday when I had started elementary school, a little girl in clothes chosen by my mother, and a warning in my head that making friends was a waste of time, a distraction from what was important about stepping out into the world.

I slept twelve, sometimes fourteen, hours a day. When I was awake, I had little energy for anything other than reading or watching reruns of TV shows that I had seen many times before. They were easy on my brain — I could repeat the conversations without watching the screen — and it seemed my brain was the part of me that needed to heal the most.

My mother didn't ask me to help her in the kitchen, but after I had been home a couple of weeks, I was feeling a little more energetic, and I wandered into the kitchen while she was preparing my favorite dumplings. I breathed in the smell of them, and watched my mother roll the dough into tiny tight balls.

"Can I help, Ma?" I asked.

She nodded and stepped aside to give me space. She didn't speak, and we worked in silence for a while, methodically filling and rolling rows of dumplings forming on the counter.

"Pa and I have been saving," she said eventually. "We can afford to send you to an Ivy League school. It is what—"

"Ma," I interrupted. "I know that's what you both want, but… I can't think about school right now."

I went back to my room and lied on my bed, staring at the ceiling. I had ruined the moment in the kitchen. For the first time in my life, I had felt like a daughter helping her mom because she wanted to and not because it was a chore demanded of her, and it had felt… nice.

But whenever I thought about school, my brain became an abyss with everything sucked out of it. I wasn't sure I would ever be able to resume my education, and I certainly believed there was no chance I would ever be accepted into an Ivy League school. My parents would have to face facts. I was a disappointment.

At night, when I was trying to read in bed, I heard the low murmur of their conversations. I couldn't hear specific words, and I wondered if they were speaking about me in low tones that wouldn't travel.

So, I was surprised when I awoke one weekend to find Joseph home. He was taller, broader, louder, and he hugged me tight when I wandered into the kitchen in my pajamas.

"Jade," he said, his voice thick with emotion, "you look great." He stood back to admire my greatness, holding me at arms' length.

I smiled. I hadn't studied my reflection since I came home, turning away from the mirror when I brushed my teeth and showering with the lights off, but now that he had said it, I realized that I felt great.

"It's Ma's cooking," I said.

"I can't wait for my first Chinese meal," said Joseph. "What are we having, Ma?"

"A banquet," said Ma. "Is that the right word?" She looked to me for confirmation, and I nodded, my cheeks coloring with emotion that my mother was still looking to me for guidance. "Our first meal all together for long while."

"And it's Thanksgiving," said Joseph.

I held my breath, waiting for her to remind him that Thanksgiving was of no importance to a traditional Chinese family, but instead, she inclined her head and said, "Yes. It is Thanksgiving."

I had noticed the way the grass outside the window had turned fiery orange with a carpet of fallen leaves; I had looked at the calendar with the picture of a scarlet Chinese dragon on it and mentally ticked off the empty days, but the celebration had skipped through my brain and barely registered as something to be aware of. It certainly had not beckoned as something to look forward to.

I saw Joseph's raised eyebrows and looked away. I did not know if my mother's acceptance was for my protection, because she did not want to trigger a reaction in me that might lead to some unpleasantness, but I was content to let it go. I could not recall a time when we had experienced such serenity between us, and I refused to be the one to spoil it.

Joseph sat in the living room with our father, while I helped Ma prepare the food. It took several hours of chopping, marinating, steaming, and frying, and although I knew that she bought the fresh ingredients from an Asian stallholder nearby, I was astounded that we were cooking so many dishes for one family meal. My shoulders tensed, waiting for the outburst about waste, and the greed of western civilization, but when it didn't come, I allowed myself to relax.

When we sat down to dinner, a pot of hot tea in the center of the table; my parents glanced at each other. Joseph was already ladling noodles onto his plate and was oblivious.

My mother cleared her throat. *Here it comes*, I thought.

"Pa and I have been saving," she said. Her eyes were on me. "We have money to send you to an Ivy

League school, Jade." I took a deep breath to speak, but she raised a hand for me to be patient and let her finish. "Why you think we work all hours? We wanted you to have the best education. Think about it, Jade. No need to make a decision right now."

Joseph squeezed my hand and smiled at me before helping himself to dumplings. "Ma's right," he said. "You don't need to do anything right now, other than get well again."

I wondered how much he knew, and whether Ma had written to him too and told him everything that had happened. But I stayed quiet.

"We wanted big money to open a restaurant," Ma said.

I stared at them, thinking I had misunderstood. Even Joseph stopped with his chopsticks halfway to his mouth.

"We not want to work for other people all our lives, and we have found a small property."

She was waiting for us to speak. Pa kept his eyes on his empty plate; he was waiting for Ma to finish.

"Wow!" said Joseph. "Where? I mean… a restaurant serving Chinese food? Do you have a business plan? Do you need me to help with that?"

"Yes," said Ma, "we do want you to help with that. Only a small restaurant in a quiet part of town where other Chinese American families live. We start small and grow big."

Joseph talked to them animatedly about business plans, and growth, and turnover, words that went over my head, not only because I didn't understand the impact of them on a business, but because playing around and around inside my head was the knowledge that our parents had been absent for so much of our childhood because they had a dream of opening a Chinese restaurant.

Did they realize that we would never be children again, that the special part of our lives when our family bonds should have been formed and strengthened, had been lost because they had been busy working and saving money?

"What do you think, Jade?" asked Joseph, jolting me back to the conversation.

"Huh?"

"You're the creative one. You could help Ma with the décor and the menu. You're the best at cooking, sorry Ma." He flashed an apologetic look at our mother. "You'll get involved while you're at home."

"Sure." I nodded. I couldn't wait to escape to my room to be left alone with my thoughts.

The following day, Joseph and I put our coats and woolly hats on and went for a walk. I loved fall. I loved the chill in the air that made my face sting, the stark trees against a backdrop of a muted sky. The shorter days and the dull skies made me feel brighter somehow, like I was the bright spark in a dull day.

"How are you feeling?" he asked eventually.

"Okay." I didn't look at him but kept my eyes on the path through the park where we were walking. "Better, anyway. I don't have to think about anything here."

I sensed his eyes on me. "Why did you do it, Jade? What happened? I mean, why didn't you speak to me, or to Ma?"

I chewed my bottom lip to prevent the tears from escaping. "Have you tried speaking to Ma about anything?" I said, ignoring the other questions.

"You could have talked to me, though. I'd have jumped on a bus and come see you if I'd known you were struggling."

I didn't say anything. I hadn't once considered calling my brother when I was curled up in my bed alone and feeling wretched, and I didn't know how we had ended up with such a distance between us.

"Did your friends not try to help?"

I thought about Lana and Aaron. They had tried getting through to me, and I had pushed them away too, consumed by my feelings of worthlessness and self-loathing.

"They tried," I said. "But… I don't know…" I shrugged. "I guess I didn't listen."

"You won't, you know, do it again, will you?" He spoke quietly as though, like Ma, he was scared of triggering a reaction in me that he would not know how to handle.

"I don't know," I said honestly.

"Why don't you let Ma and Pa pay for you to go to a different school? Start afresh. New courses, new friends."

"I don't want to be a pharmacist, Joseph. I never did want to."

I wanted to tell him about the band, but I still couldn't find the words to explain how I had even let myself down with the one thing that was important to me.

"Who said you would have to be a pharmacist? Get some qualifications behind you, and then go sing in a cabaret club if that's what makes you happy."

"Ha!" I snapped. "Ma would never allow that to happen."

"You know, Jade," he said, "for an intelligent girl, you can be such an idiot sometimes."

I looked at him, and he grinned at me.

"What do you mean?"

"How could they stop you? All they ever wanted was for you to have something to fall back on should you need a change of career. Something solid, dependable. And all you've ever done is get angry with them."

I stopped in my tracks, my breath catching in my throat. I'd never looked at it from anyone else's perspective. Now I realized why Joseph had gone along with everything that our parents had planned for him without ever questioning it. I'd assumed that it was different for him, easier because he was a boy, but it wasn't that at all. He had it all worked out. He'd gone through childhood with the right attitude that, whichever path he took, he needed to ensure a decent future for himself.

I nodded and kept walking. It was something else to think about when I was in my room later, staring at the ceiling.

"You didn't have much to say about Ma's announcement yesterday," he said.

"I—I couldn't help thinking that they should have worked less when we were growing up. How much time did they spend with us, Joseph? I mean, actually spend with us, asking us about school, about friends, taking us out to baseball games the way other families do?"

"We're not like other families," he said. "They came here with a dream, and they put their dream to one side so that they could give us an easier life. What's so wrong with that?"

What was so wrong with that?

I wasn't sure I knew the answer.

Chapter Twenty-Nine

There was an apartment above the restaurant that my parents purchased. It was small, compact, but it felt brighter, lighter than our house ever had. My room overlooked a kindergarten behind the back, which was next to a small play area, so the sounds of children playing and squealing with excitement could be heard throughout the day.

There were only two bedrooms, and my parents would sleep on a sofa bed in the living room whenever Joseph came to stay, so that he and I could still each have a room. Ma asked my opinion on paint colors and allowed me to decorate the rooms as I was taking a break from my studies.

I guessed she was trying to keep me busy to keep my mind from anything that might send me spiraling down into depression, but also, she'd always been more practical than creative. I painted my room sunny yellow. I hung white curtains with a large daisy print on the window, and hand-painted tiny bobbing daisies on the walls; it made me smile whenever I walked into the room.

My father was busy with the financial aspect of the business. I was surprised — I had never given him any credit for anything other than being a manual grafter, but he seemed to know what he was doing, and questioned anything that didn't appear to work in their favor.

When it came to the restaurant, my mother gave me free rein to choose the décor, paint colors, fixtures, and accessories. I spent hours poring over paint colors in hardware stores. I visited soft furnishings stores and, in the evenings, I went with Ma to other restaurants, where we compared the interiors with our own ideas, scribbling notes in a notepad about what worked and what didn't work, brainstorming ideas until we agreed on a color scheme and theme that we were both happy with.

We'd decided to stick to a traditional Chinese theme with dragons and lanterns and large fans on the walls, but instead of the traditional crimson and gold, we adapted the theme to shades of green and copper and burnt gold to reflect my favorite season. With the restaurant itself decorated, and the hard furnishings installed, it became my new favorite place to be.

We had floor-to-ceiling trees stenciled onto the walls, and it was like walking into a forest but without the sounds of the bird chirping in the trees. It gave me a sense of peace the way nothing else ever had. I began to forget all about school, and graduation, and even singing in a band, as the restaurant consumed my thoughts.

In my spare time, I lied on my bed, physically exhausted, and studied the Chinese horoscope. I was born in the year of the horse, and my horoscope told me that this year was a time of great change for me, with new paths leading me in directions I might not have previously considered.

It was growing close to Chinese New Year, which was when my parents planned the grand opening of the restaurant. It looked like a restaurant now, but quite unlike any we had visited, a mixture of Chinese and American, traditional and modern, and my chest swelled with pride whenever I sat in one of the secluded booths. All that was left to do was hire some help, and we were almost ready.

Joseph returned for the opening night. Together, Ma and I had produced a simple but elegant menu, offering a smaller range of our best dishes, prepared using locally-sourced food where possible. We decided to open with a buffet banquet and bottles of champagne, to introduce customers to the kind of meals we would offer moving forward.

Ma had employed a young waiter named Lim, who was helping Joseph and I serve the food while Ma and Pa, dressed in fancy new clothes, greeted customers and introduced themselves.

The first customers arrived within minutes of the doors being opened, and we were kept busy until we closed later that evening. Joseph and Lim were the perfect servers, sharp in white shirts with brocade waistcoats that matched the cool green décor piped with gold trim. I helped Ma in the kitchen, and when things were under control, helped out in the restaurant, where I saw my father mingling with customers, a rare smile lighting up his face. I had never heard my father speak so much in my entire life.

At the end of the evening, when the last customers had gone, Ma and Pa slumped heavily onto seats in one of the booths and beckoned the three of us to join them. Pa filled champagne flutes with bubbly liquid, and we all raised a glass to toast the success of our opening night.

"Cheers," said Joseph. "I would call this a successful opening night."

We clinked glasses, and my finger brushed against Lim's. I quickly pulled my hand away and deliberately looked in my mother's direction so that he would not know that I felt it. Lim was good-looking, but I didn't understand why he still went by his Asian name. Did he not want to fit in?

He was talking about families and teamwork and saying how he loved the way we all pulled together. I chewed my bottom lip and kept my eyes on my glass. If he only knew. For the first time, I was conscious of my scars and grateful that Ma had chosen long-sleeved white shirts as part of our matching outfits, and now I crossed my arms over my chest as though I could make the worst scar disappear.

"Lim is studying art at college," said Ma.

"You are?" I didn't know why I was so surprised. I'd assumed that Lim was still at school, but I think I was even more shocked to discover that he was studying art. "Not science? Are your parents okay with that?"

I blurted out without thinking, and my face grew hot as I realized what I'd said. I saw Joseph's brief shake of his head as though he couldn't believe I'd not listened to him when we had our chat.

"Science, also," said Lim, "but I'm good at art, and they didn't want me to waste my talent."

I sipped champagne and made a mental note to consider this when I was alone in my sunny yellow room upstairs.

Ma left the table and returned with some sticky chicken wings, and salt and pepper prawns, piled onto a dish.

"We not waste food," she said.

We were quiet while we ate, and Lim was the first to speak again. "These are delicious, Ma." He licked sauce from his fingers, his eyes bright from the bubbles.

"Jade made them," said Ma, smiling. "She learn from the best."

We all laughed at Ma's joke; it was the first time in my life I had heard my mother say something funny, and I could not stop the grin from staying on my face.

The restaurant became our life. I remembered Thanksgiving, when our parents had first mentioned their dream of opening a restaurant, and how angry I had been with them for wasting our childhood working. But now, when I tried to recreate the anger inside me, I struggled to locate the source of it.

I had never seen my parents so happy, even though they were working longer hours now than they ever had. Ma woke up early, before sunrise, to begin preparing food, while Pa traveled to markets to find the freshest local produce. They both worked in the kitchen all day, and then in the evenings, they worked in the restaurant until it closed.

But it was more than that. They had a dream which they had finally fulfilled, and I knew that I was wrong to be angry about it. It was only right that I was here to help them achieve it in any way I could. I had a dream, too. Sure, it was on hold right now, but my parents were proof that this didn't mean it was over.

Winter turned to spring, and spring warmed enough for the trees to grow new shoots and the flowers to blossom, and we filled tiny pots on each table in the restaurant with delicate pink blooms. I needed to think about college, but I still wasn't sure that I was ready to go back. I felt safe here in Ma's kitchen, safe and comfortable, and I no longer felt stifled by my family's presence or demands. I helped Ma willingly, and in return, she did not push me to reapply to college.

Aaron and I exchanged letters frequently. He was still singing with the band — they had a few more gigs, nothing huge, but he was enjoying it. They still missed me, he said, but I tried not to dwell on it. I'd let them down; they did not owe me anything. He never mentioned Sam in his correspondence, and for that, I was grateful. He was thrilled to hear about the restaurant and said that he would visit as soon as college finished for the summer, and he came home to his folks. I was nervous about seeing him, especially when I thought about the almost-kiss, but excited too.

Lim and I had grown closer. He attended college locally, which was why he was able to work in his spare time, and he showed me some of his artwork. I was impressed. He was so talented that it was unthinkable that he would not achieve his dream to be a fashion designer.

One day, he came to the apartment when Ma was downstairs working in the kitchen, and I was taking a break. He had brought an outfit with him — one of his own designs. It was a dress: the skirt was sheer black and flared out from the waist in stiff folds, with a slinky black underskirt that clung to my hips, and a figure-hugging black bodice piped with amber silk.

It tried it on and stared at my reflection in the mirror. I looked amazing.

"Perfect," said Lim.

"Oh my god," I said. "How did you know it would look this good? How did you know my size?"

"It wasn't difficult," he said. "We spend a lot of time together."

I nodded. I could not take my eyes off my reflection wearing this dress. I pictured myself on a stage in front of a small audience, singing the song Aaron and I had written a lifetime ago, and it somehow felt as though it had been someone else's dream, in another world where dreams come true.

My expression must have changed because Lim said, "Ma says that you sing."

My reflection watched him. "She did?"

He nodded. "My college has a great music course."

I glanced back at myself, at the dress that made me look like someone else, someone who didn't hurt herself when things got rough.

"I don't know if I'm ready to go back," I murmured. "The restaurant…"

It was a feeble excuse. Ma and Pa would cope without me.

"I'm still here." He shrugged. When he smiled, I could see his perfect white teeth, and something inside me ignited like a match being struck. "You could still help out during weekends and evenings. Think about it, Jade. If you're as good as Ma says you are, what's stopping you?"

Chapter Thirty

I was slicing mushrooms in the restaurant kitchen, which overlooked the small vegetable garden Pa had planted with Joseph's help over the summer. We grew carrots and cabbages and onions, and Pa had built a greenhouse to grow tomatoes. I could hear children in the park, squealing and yelling as they played on the swings and kicked a ball around.

"You need to get ready," said Ma.

She was preparing spices, the wok ready to start frying. The kitchen was already filled with the warm spicy aroma that reminded me of my childhood, afternoons spent helping Ma prepare dinner after school, the radio tuned into the Chinese station that Ma was still listening to now.

"I'll go upstairs and change in a minute," I said.

Lim appeared in the doorway, already dressed in his waiter's outfit which he had customized over the summer to include his Chinese horoscope animal: the dragon.

"Jade, you should be getting ready," he said.

"You sound like Ma." I smiled at him over my shoulder, but I stopped anyway and rinsed my hands under the faucet. "I'm going now."

He grinned, making his eyebrows dance comically. "It's busy."

"Are you trying to make me nervous?"

"No, I'm trying to tell you that everyone knows you're going to be great."

I couldn't help but smile at him. We'd spent the summer together, when we weren't working, visiting museums and libraries, and exploring the surrounding area. We visited the Liberty Bell. We went fishing. We even took a bus to New York and wandered around Central Park and Macy's, and admired the windows of the designer stores on Fifth Avenue.

Lim said he would live there one day in a penthouse apartment, with his own store on one of the avenues where famous people would wait six months for him to create an unforgettable outfit for them.

"And I'll be singing to a packed audience at Madison Square," I said.

I no longer believed in the dream, but it seemed that Lim did.

I applied to the same college as Lim, on a music degree that would allow me to focus on my voice while also learning to play guitar. My parents didn't question my decision or push for me to attend an Ivy League school; I think they were simply relieved that I had returned to my studies at all after what happened at Lehigh.

Lim and I still worked together some evenings and weekends when our studies allowed, but it was our personal time that I looked forward to more than anything else. We had kissed a couple of times, and it had been gentle, romantic, the way I had expected Aaron's kisses to feel, had we ever gotten around to seeing it through. It wasn't something I dwelled on anymore. If it was meant to be, it would've happened no matter what, regardless of my short-lived obsession with Sam.

I still thought of Sam occasionally. Whenever I did, my heart would begin to race, my breathing becoming shallow, not because of any overwhelming attraction to him, or a great sense of loss, but simply because those feelings were associated with memories of despair.

I had learned to accept that it might take years for those feelings to disappear or become controllable, or that they might always be there, a part of me as plain as the nose on my face or my chestnut brown hair, but they no longer controlled me or upset me. They came, and they passed, and I was okay.

Upstairs in my room, I changed out of my kitchen clothes and stepped into the black dress that Lim created for me. I did my makeup, glossy red lips, a touch of amber above my eyes, a flick of eyeliner in each corner, and smiled at my reflection.

Downstairs, I could hear the hum of conversation from the restaurant. Lim had convinced my parents to construct a small stage in one corner of the room so that we could provide entertainment some evenings. The stage was raised with arched wooden bridges leading to it, resembling a Chinese garden, and the disco evenings we had trialed with a resident

DJ had proven popular with customers who had an occasion to celebrate. The stage was usually filled with people dancing and singing after their meal, and we were taking bookings months in advance.

Tonight though, the stage was being used for a different occasion. Tonight, I was performing a new song that I had written, and some other favorites that I had loved to sing with Aaron. Waiting in the hallway, I smoothed my dress, and took some deep breaths, in through my nose and out through my mouth, to regulate my heartbeat.

Lim appeared and took my hands in his. "You look amazing," he said. "Good enough to kiss."

I shook my head. "You'll smudge my lipstick."

"Later then." He watched me eagerly, eyes wide and bright.

I nodded. "Later."

My mother stepped out from the kitchen, wiping her hands on a dish towel. "Jade, you look beautiful." There were tears in her eyes, and she swallowed hard. "I am so proud of you."

I smiled at my mother. I had been shocked when they told me that Lim suggested I should sing at the restaurant, and even more shocked when I heard that they had agreed. Since then, my mother encouraged me to sing in the kitchen, and she occasionally sung along with me to the popular songs that she recognized. I knew that she still hoped I would eventually graduate from college and settle down with a sensible job that would provide me with a stable future, but we only spoke about it if I raised the subject, which I rarely did.

"Thanks, Ma," I said. I blew her a kiss, and she caught it in her hand.

I stepped out onto the stage and glanced around the restaurant. Joseph was standing by the entrance, wearing his server's outfit. He winked at me, and I was flooded with affection. Some friends from college were seated in booths, and they cheered and whooped as our eyes met, and I readied the mic.

In another booth, Aaron was sitting with Lana. They had been dating for a while now, on and off, and I was pleased to see that they were holding hands. They both waved at me, and I nodded at them. They had looked out for me when I needed them the most, and I was happy that they had found each other; maybe I was meant to bring them together all along.

I raised the mic to my lips. "Hello, everyone," I said. "Thank you for coming. My name is Yù, but you can call me Jade."

Chapter Thirty-One

The day I graduated, the sun was shining, and the world had come alive, like it had just woken from a particularly restful nap. It had rained during the night, and everything was sparkling, scoured clean and fresh, the grass springy underfoot. It felt, not like the end of college, but like a new beginning. I was graduating! Me, Jade Xiu, I'd made it through college a year later than I should have, but it didn't matter; it was the journey that was important.

The restaurant was well established now and thriving. Ma and Pa still worked six days a week, closing on Mondays, which gave them a chance to visit local markets, tweak the menu, prepare batches of sauces and spices in advance, and listen to Chinese music, the same radio station they'd been listening to since they moved to America.

Ma had taken on another woman, Xiao, to help in the kitchen. She was older than Ma and had come across from China several years before my parents, but her grasp of the English language was still minimal, and her Chinese accent almost unrecognizable so that I had to wait for Ma to translate whenever I was helping out. Xiao was messy — I often heard Ma complaining about the hours she spent cleaning the kitchen — but her food was incomparable.

Lim and I were dating. It was a gradual thing that we drifted into after our first kiss and when I first applied to attend the same college, but now it felt as though there had been a space by my side all along that was waiting to be filled by him. I couldn't imagine not being around him. My parents loved him, and even Joseph treated him like a brother whenever he was home. I had achieved everything I had ever wanted, and when I looked back on high school and the few months I spent at Lehigh, it was difficult to recall why I had felt so weighted down by life.

My friends were like toddlers on the first day of kindergarten, jumping about, fiddling with their hair, and squealing every time someone spoke. Their excitement was contagious, but I felt an inner peace that I had cultivated over the last few years with Lim, a way of detaching myself from whatever was going on around me and focusing on the feel of the clothes on my skin, the sunshine on my cheeks, the shoes on my feet. I practiced this now, concentrating on my breathing, in through my nose one… two… three, and out through my mouth one… two… three. It helped.

I watched as people arrived and took their seats on the field surrounding the stage, where we would be presented with our diplomas. It reminded me of my first performance in *West Side Story* at high school, peeking out from behind the curtains with Jen, knowing that my family would not be there to hear me sing. I still felt a twinge of sadness for thirteen-year-old Jade Xiu who had no clue what the future held for her, because here she was, about to graduate knowing that everyone she loved in the world would be there to watch.

Part of me wished I could turn back the clock and tell young Jade that it would be okay. Another part of me understood that the decisions I made when I was growing up were necessary; they helped make me the girl I am today, and I should never want to change a thing.

I spotted Joseph and his girlfriend, Lisa, first. They had been seeing each other for two years now, and she was lovely. She reminded me a little of Jen, who I saw occasionally around town — blonde, pretty, bubbly, probably the complete opposite of the wife my parents would have chosen for their only son, but they had welcomed her into our home and into our hearts, and I was happy for my brother.

They took their seats, and Joseph nodded at me when our eyes met. Lim took a seat next to Joseph. Beautiful, kind, generous Lim. He smiled at me, and I lit up inside. It wasn't long before my parents joined them, my father with streaks of silver in his hair, my mother with her face expressionless until she saw me and gave a shy wave.

Bonnie, the girl beside me, shrieked when she saw her mom arriving with her grandparents, and I was distracted watching the way they smiled and waved at each other, until the dean took the podium and announced the commencement of the graduation ceremony.

Butterflies turned somersaults inside my stomach as he spoke, excited at the thought of my parents watching me graduate and knowing there must have been a time when they would have wondered if it would ever happen. I was grateful to have been given a second chance and to prove to them that I was the good Chinese daughter they always wanted me to be.

When it was my turn, I mounted the stage and accepted my diploma, shaking hands with the dean, and turning to smile at my family. Lim blew me a kiss, his grin wide. My mom dabbed her eyes with a tissue. And then I left the stage at the other side and waited for it to be over.

So, it wasn't until the families and friends in the audience were rising to meet us, that I noticed the way my father helped my mother to her feet, the way Joseph fussed over her, taking her elbow and guiding her along the row of seats, the way her bones protruded through her clothes, which looked two sizes too large. Her face was gray. Lim was watching me watching her, an unfathomable expression on his face, and suddenly I knew.

Chapter Thirty-Two

I t was incurable.
She had never smoked a cigarette in her life, but cancer had attacked her lungs with frightening velocity and then, having devoured what it could, had spread to her liver, kidneys, and spine. They had known for a while, but they wanted me to graduate before they told me. I had suffered enough at Lehigh

for them to be determined not to jinx my education this time around.

"You should have told me, Ma," I said.

She was in bed the day after my graduation, and Xiao was running the kitchen. My mother hadn't even complained about how much mess she would discover later, and that was when it hit me how sick she really was. It was the first time I had ever seen her in bed. It was the first time I had ever set foot in their room in my entire life, and it saddened me how little they had in the way of possessions. As a child, I'd been angry about not having a princess canopy over my bed or posters on my wall, and my parents had nothing, not even a shade to cover the overhead lamp.

"I wanted you to graduate, Jade," she said. "You worked so hard for it. I could not take that away from you. When I'm gone, you—"

"No!" I snapped. "Don't say that. You'll get better. You need to think positive, Ma. None of this negative stuff, okay?"

I fussed around her bed, straightening the cover over her frighteningly skinny legs, plumping the pillows, holding a cup to her lips so that she could sip some water. She watched me, her eyes moving slowly around in her frozen face.

"I'm going to check on the kitchen downstairs," I said. "I'll bring some soup up for you. It'll make you feel better."

She lied back with her eyes closed, and a wave of fear swept over me — one day, she would close her eyes and never open them again. I stood by the bed trembling, my heart beating a strange tune as though it wasn't sure whether it should still be working.

"Ma?" My voice trembled, too.

Her eyes flickered open, and she gave me a half-smile and a nod before she closed them again.

I left the room, closing the door behind me, and stood there listening while I waited for my heartbeat to regulate. This could not be happening. She had always been so filled with energy, so active, so there, it was impossible to comprehend that her body was shutting down. Yesterday was my graduation, and the world had been filled with sunshine, and today... today felt as though fifty years had passed overnight, draining my mother of her life-force.

She should not have told me. She should not have spoken the words aloud. If they hadn't entered the universe, none of this would be happening, and today would have been like any other day.

I went downstairs to the kitchen where Xiao was busy slicing vegetables on a chopping board, her back to me as I entered. Through the window, I saw my father in the vegetable garden, his back bowed. He looked smaller too, frailer. They had both aged overnight, and it occurred to me that my father had spent his entire adult life with my mother, and he would not know what to do without her.

Xiao must have sensed me watching. "Soup."

She nodded to a tureen on the counter.

I ladled some into a bowl and took a spoon from the cutlery drawer. There were some daisies in a jar on the windowsill, something that my mother had continued since the first time I brought flowers home. I took the jar and placed it onto a tray beside the soup. In the garden, my father had straightened, but he did not turn around and look back at us, and I wondered if he was crying.

Xiao reached for my hand and squeezed it. She didn't say anything but peered into my eyes, and I knew from her silence, that she was telling me to be strong, to be the good Chinese daughter my mother always wanted me to be.

My father barely spoke. He spent all his time downstairs in his office at the back of the restaurant, poring over numbers and scribbling in a huge wide ledger that was permanently open on his desk. Joseph came and went. He was staying with Lisa's family because they had a large house with spare rooms, and they had welcomed Joseph with open arms. He was at medical school studying to be a surgeon, but he still played football and was fit and strong — he would make Lisa a great husband one day. But around our mother, he clammed up like a snail inside its shell and could barely even look at her without bawling.

Because my mother was in Joseph's room, I made my father sleep in my room. He needed to rest. He needed to keep the restaurant running smoothly, because overnight, my mother's illness had consumed her to the point where she had left the bed for the last time.

I sat with her. During the day, I spoon-fed her soup — it was all that she could swallow other than a few sips of green tea or cooled boiled water. I washed her with hot towels. I changed her clothes, sitting her forward and raising her arms one at a time like a newborn baby. I dabbed her cracked lips with cotton buds soaked in water.

At night, I slept in a chair by the side of her bed. We didn't talk, but we didn't need to; she knew that I was there, and that was all that mattered.

Sometimes I sang to her, songs that I had written myself.

I had taken up the guitar as naturally as feeding myself and had performed at a few small gigs around the area. I still wanted to be a singer, but I no longer stressed over when or how it would happen — I had learned that if I was determined to succeed, and I persevered with following my dream, it *would* happen. When I sang, a smile touched the corners of her lips, and I knew that she was peaceful.

Lim came every day. He sat with her while I showered, or helped Xiao in the kitchen, or went out to buy more flowers, and whenever I saw his smile, I was grateful all over again to have him in my life. I wondered if that was how my parents felt when they gazed into each other's eyes — grateful. Was that enough after a lifetime together? Or did they want more?

There was so much I wanted to tell my mother, but I didn't even know where to start, and the days dragged on in comfortable silence, me pottering around the room, and my mother's eyes closed apart from when I was feeding or bathing her. Then she would look at me, wide-eyed, and I was frightened of the fear I saw behind the fading color, so I would hide it by saying, "Are you comfortable, Ma? Have you had enough soup? Are your lips dry?" without looking at her.

One time, Lim gestured for me to step outside the room with him as he was leaving. "Are you okay, Jade?" he asked.

I nodded. "I'm fine."

"You look tired. You should get some rest. Do you want me to take over tonight so that you can sleep?"

I shrank away from him as if I had already spent too long away from her. "No. No, I can't leave her."

"Hey," he said, squeezing my hand. "You've done everything you could. She knows you have."

Tears welled in my eyes. "Most of the time, she doesn't even know I'm there. Her eyes are closed."

He smiled at me. "She knows you're there, Jade. I can see it on her face, even if she does look like she is sleeping."

Tears streaked my face, and I didn't wipe them away. I swallowed. "She doesn't have long, does she?"

He shook his head. "No, but I don't think there is anyone else she would rather be with." He was quiet for a few moments. "You should tell her how you feel." I went to shake my head, and he continued, "I know you don't like to speak about your emotions, and I know you were never close to her when you were younger, but if you're ever going to tell her that you love her, now is the time."

I nodded. I waited outside the room for a long while after Lim left, thinking about what to say, but no sentences would form inside my head. In the end, I went back inside and sat on my chair by the bed.

I took my mother's hand in mine and held it gently. Her hand was icy cold, frail, as light as cradling a bird in my hand.

"Ma," I whispered. "It's me, Yù. I don't know if you can hear me, but I want to tell you… I want to tell you that I love you. I may not have always been the best daughter, and I know that sometimes I upset you when I complained about Chinese New Year and the Dragon Festival, but… but secretly I loved our Chinese heritage. I still do. I love being a part of this culture, but I also love being American. I've realized that it doesn't have to be one or the other, it can be both; there never was any need for me to choose between the two. I will never ever forget where you came from and what you taught me, Ma. I will teach my own children to embrace being Chinese American, and I will tell them that I learned from the best. I learned from you, Ma."

I leaned closer and kissed my mother on the lips as I whispered my final goodbye.

Struggle
Between
Two Lives

Struggle
Between
Two Lives